THE SIGN OF THE CROOKED ARROW

The HARDY BOYS *Mystery Stories*
BY FRANKLIN W. DIXON

Frank flattened out to make himself as inconspicuous
a target as possible

The Sign of the Crooked Arrow

THE SIGN OF
THE CROOKED ARROW

BY

FRANKLIN W. DIXON

NEW YORK
GROSSET & DUNLAP
Publishers

CONTENTS

THE SIGN OF THE CROOKED ARROW

CHAPTER I

The Mysterious Car

THE Hardy boys' new club coupé, heading for the open country, whizzed past a road sign inscribed *Bayport City Limits*.

Frank, the elder brother, fingered the wheel lightly. Joe sat beside him, his blond hair whipping in the breeze.

"What's all this business about somebody forgetting a car?" Joe asked.

"A man and his wife left it at Slow Mo's garage in Pleasantville two months ago and never called for it," Frank replied.

The boys' father, Detective Fenton Hardy, had given Frank the details of the case and suggested that his sons follow it up. The garage proprietor had appealed to him to find the owner of the car.

"Why didn't Slow Mo contact the license bureau?" Joe put in.

1

"Dad asked him that. When Slow Mo went to look at the plates, they were gone!"

"Who took 'em off?"

"That's what we're to find out," Frank said. "It seems they were stolen."

"Sounds like a good case." Joe grinned. "One thing's sure: the car owner wouldn't take them."

"Strike one," Frank agreed. "It sounds as if Slow Mo might be in a jam."

Half an hour later Frank pulled up in front of a rickety building in the sleepy town of Pleasantville.

"That must be Slow Mo," Frank declared, as an elderly man in overalls shuffled toward them.

"Hello, boys," he said. "What can I do for you?" When he learned who they were, he asked in surprise, "Where's your pop?"

"He's busy on another case," Joe replied. "He sent us to help you."

The old man frowned. "I sure wanted your pop to figure this thing out. He's the best detective in this part of the country."

"You're right there," said Frank. "But I think we can make a start on solving the mystery. We often work with Dad on cases."

Slow Mo, who had been dubbed Slow Motion in his youth, rubbed his whiskers with a grimy finger. He was a man of medium height, but he looked taller because of a thatch of bristling gray hair which stuck up on top of his head like a paint brush.

"Well, I dunno," he said. "But come in my office and I'll tell you what happened, anyway."

"What do the police think?" Frank asked him, as they followed.

"Didn't ask the police," Slow Mo said. "Jake, the chief—he's my brother-in-law—ain't solved a case in thirty years. That's why I called your pop."

The old man crossed the floor of the musty-smelling garage and entered a two-by-four room. It was stacked high with empty oil cans and old tires.

On the wall hung a faded calendar dating back years. It was the only calendar in the place. Slow Mo had kept it, he said, because he liked the fisherman pictured on it.

"Haven't you a calendar for this year?" Frank queried.

Slow Mo gave a sheepish smile. "Never thought of that," he said.

"Where's your office?" Joe asked with a wink at Frank.

"Why, gol hang it, boy," Slow Mo said, "I can see right now you're not the detective your father is. This is the office. He'd of knowed that right off."

"Sorry," Joe replied, keeping a straight face.

"Set down here," the proprietor offered, motioning toward a couple of kegs.

The brothers seated themselves as Slow Mo unfolded his story. Most of it they already knew. At one point Joe interrupted to ask for a description of the couple who had left the car.

Slow Mo looked blank for a moment, then said, "Why, they're kinda ordinary-lookin' folks, middlin' height, dressed like reg'lar people—"

Joe shook his head. Slow Mo's description would apply to a million other strangers!

"Where did the couple go after they left their car?" Frank asked.

"Took a train from here," Slow Mo replied. "Station's right over there," he said, pointing.

Pleasantville's one pride was being the terminal of a railroad spur. It served several towns along its route to Bayport.

"What's the engine number of the car?" Frank quizzed.

"Why, I dunno," Slow Mo answered. "Guess I should 'a' looked at it. Never thought of that."

He led the Hardys to the rear of the garage, where a black sedan stood in a corner.

Frank threw up the hood of the automobile and glanced at the engine.

"Got a flashlight?" he asked Slow Mo.

When the proprietor handed him one, Frank scanned the motor.

"Just as I thought!" he exclaimed. "The engine number has been filed off."

"What would anybody do that for?" Slow Mo asked, running his fingers through his bristle top.

"To conceal the identity of the car," Frank explained. "This," he added, "is a case for the local police chief, whether you like him or not."

Slow Mo telephoned him. Soon afterward a short, fat man puffed into the garage.

"Hello, Jake," Slow Mo said. "These are the Hardy boys. Sons of Fenton Hardy, the detective."

"What have they done?" Jake asked. "Want 'em arrested?"

"No," Frank said, laughing. "We'd like you to arrest the person who filed the number off the engine of this car." He pointed to the mysterious black sedan.

"Besides, the guy that left it here owes me two months' rent," put in Slow Mo.

An eager look spread over Police Chief Jake's face. His nose grew red and his eyes narrowed as he wiped his shiny bald head with a bright bandanna handkerchief.

"I'll arrest him, all right. Where is he?"

"That's what we'd like to find out," Frank said. "Slow Mo said he left here two months ago."

"Got a head start, didn't he?" Jake reasoned. "But I'll get him."

Jake blew his nose three times, like an elephant trumpeting for his mate, then looked inside the car.

"Stand back now, boys," he said, "while I look for some clues."

Joe smothered a laugh when the chief pulled a big magnifying glass from his back pocket. The officer seemed interested only in what lay on the surface of the car. After a five-minute study he said gravely:

"I think this car was stolen." Then he added with authority, "I'll send out a seven-state alarm." With that the chief puffed out of the building.

"Guess that does it," Slow Mo said with a shrug.

"Does what?" asked Joe.

"Solves the case," Slow Mo replied. "Just like he solves all the cases in Pleasantville; not at all."

Frank spoke up. "If that's true, suppose Joe and I look for some clues."

"Sure, go ahead," the garage owner said.

Frank started a systematic study of the car's upholstery, while his brother removed the mats from the front and rear floors. Presently, from inside the front compartment, which otherwise was empty, Joe drew out a narrow leather strap. It was worn at one end.

"Looks like part of an old strap from a wrist watch," he commented, showing it to Frank. "Wonder why anyone would save it."

"It may be a valuable clue," his brother said.

He himself continued to probe the cushions. He

pulled out the back seat and ran his hand behind the upholstery. His reward was a hairpin and a ten-cent piece. Then suddenly his fingers tightened around a strange object. Tugging carefully, the boy pulled out an ornamental piece of jewelry.

"A tie clasp," Frank announced, holding the object in his palm.

"It's an arrow, but it's crooked," Joe observed.

Slow Mo peered closely at the slightly S-shaped arrow tie clasp. "Probably got bent," he said, "when somebody sat on it."

"I don't think so," Frank replied. "It looks to me as if it were made that way."

Pocketing the piece of strap and the tie clasp, the Hardys said good-bye to Slow Mo and left the garage. Joe got behind the wheel for the trip home and Frank slid in beside him. Just as Joe was about to press the starter button, a rough-looking man turned in from the road and walked into the garage.

"I wonder who that guy is?" Joe asked. "Looks like a prize fighter."

Frank and Joe waited a moment. They heard the men's voices from inside, arguing loudly.

"We'd better see what's the matter," Frank said. "Sounds as if Slow Mo's in trouble."

The brothers got out of their car and started inside. As they did, the stranger snarled at Slow Mo:

"All right, I didn't leave it! And I don't care if the license plates are gone. I'm taking this car!"

With that he gave Slow Mo a wallop. The elderly garage owner staggered backward and fell.

His head struck the concrete floor with a resounding crack and he sprawled unconscious.

CHAPTER II

Daylight Robbery

FRANK and Joe rushed forward. The burly stranger, surprised by their sudden entrance, halted abruptly. Then he whirled about and raced out the side door of the garage.

While Frank bent over Slow Mo, his brother tore after the man, who made a beeline for the railroad station.

Both boys were now certain that they had stumbled onto a real case. The youths, still in high school, had started solving mysteries when one they later called "The Tower Treasure" had come their way.

Since then they had been doing detective work not only in the Bayport ¦area where they lived but in other places as well. Recently they had discovered the reason for the mysterious water shortage in town, but only after some narrow escapes, while solving "The Secret of Skull Mountain."

Now Joe was running after a man who gave every evidence of being involved in some crooked dealing. The boy was only a few yards behind him as he raced up the wooden steps of the old Pleasantville station, three at a time. At that moment a train was pulling out.

With a lunge, the man grasped the handrail on the last coach, teetered precariously a moment, then pulled himself aboard. By this time the train was moving fast.

Joe missed his man by inches. In disgust, he returned to the garage and told Frank, who was bathing Slow Mo's head with cold water.

"How is he?" Joe asked.

"He's coming to," Frank replied.

As the boys watched, Slow Mo's eyelids fluttered and opened.

"Wh-where am I?" he asked in a daze.

"In your office," Frank replied. "Take it easy."

"I remember now," the man said. "Big guy hit me. Where'd he go? Did he get the car?"

When Frank told him the mysterious stranger had escaped, but without the car, Slow Mo breathed a sigh of relief.

"I'm glad he got away. He might have hurt you boys. I wouldn't want anything to happen to Fenton Hardy's sons on my account."

Assured that Slow Mo was well enough to be left

the boys drove off to the police station to tell Chief Jake what had happened.

"I'll send out a seven-state alarm," the officer puffed. "Nobody can come to Pleasantville and sock my brother-in-law!"

A few minutes later Frank and Joe left the police station and headed back to Bayport.

"I don't like the looks of this, Joe," Frank said, frowning.

His brother agreed. "What's your guess? Think it really is that man's car?"

"No. Probably trying to collect it for the fellow who left it."

"Then why the big rush to get out of the garage? I'll bet he was trying to steal the car!"

"What I want to know," Frank declared, "is who took the license plates and obliterated the engine number."

All the way back to Bayport the brothers tried vainly to figure out what was back of the mystery. "Perhaps Dad can," Joe said as they reached home and entered the Hardy driveway.

The boys hurried into their father's study and found him seated in a red leather chair poring over a dossier of criminal records. When his sons entered, the detective laid the papers aside.

"Hello, boys," he said. "How did you make out at Slow Mo's?"

Joe turned a chair around and straddled it, while Frank sat on the edge of his father's desk. Mr. Hardy knew something unusual was in the air.

"Well, tell me," he urged. "Have you two run into something hot?"

"Dad," Frank said seriously, "there's something crooked about that abandoned car out at Slow Mo's place."

Fenton Hardy raised his eyebrows and sat forward in his chair. Frank told his story, then showed his father the worn watch strap and the crooked arrow tie clasp.

"What do you make of it, Dad?" Joe asked impatiently.

"Boys," replied Mr Hardy, "I believe you've dug up some clues which may tie in with a case I'm working on; a very baffling case."

"What's that?" Frank put in, amazed.

"You've been reading about the wave of robberies in and about Bayport, haven't you?"

The boys nodded as the detective went on. "The Businessmen's Association has engaged me to apprehend the criminals. They think the police are a bit slow," he said, smiling.

"The *Bayport Times* believes an out-of-town gang is committing the robberies," Frank said.

"Yes, I know, but I don't agree with the *Times*," replied his father. "I'll admit it does look as if a mob of thugs might be at the bottom of it, because each of the thieves answers to a different description. In fact, that's the police theory. But I feel there's a marked similarity to each of the crimes, and there may be one person directing the whole thing."

"A ring of thieves isn't usually so large anyway, is it?" Frank asked.

"Exactly," Mr. Hardy said. "Thieves operate alone or in small groups. Otherwise, there would be too many to share the loot."

"Are these papers the records of the robberies?" Joe asked, pointing to the sheaf on the desk.

"Yes," the detective replied. "They're statements from the victims, which include bank tellers, cashiers in stores, and citizens robbed on the street while carrying large sums of money. I find that in each case the same thing happened. Immediately after the victims had been accosted, they became faint and lost consciousness. They woke up a few minutes later, minus whatever of value they had with them."

"What made them faint?" Joe asked.

"That's what I'm working to find out," was Mr. Hardy's answer. "The victims were not held up, in the true sense, but it's evident to me that in every instance the man who stopped and asked a question was one of the thieves."

"What did they ask?"

"Various things; what time it was, where a certain bus stopped, or in several cases for a match to light a cigarette."

"Dad," Frank put in, "what makes you think this case of yours ties in with the mystery of the car at Slow Mo's?"

Fenton Hardy smiled. "The crooked arrow tie clasp," he said. "The only clue I've picked up in my case was from a recording machine I concealed in a cheap restaurant on the water front called Mike's Place. It's known as a hangout for shady characters. Someone used the words "crooked arrow."

"Crooked arrow?" Joe repeated. "What do you think it means?"

Mr. Hardy shrugged. "Maybe a symbol or sign of a gang."

Just then a tall, angular woman strode through the doorway of the detective's study.

"Hello, Aunt Gertrude," said the boys, rising and offering her a chair.

"Hello," she replied, then blurted out, "Shame on you, Fenton Hardy! I just heard you talking about a new case. So that's why you're not going out West to help our poor cousin Ruth!"

Aunt Gertrude, Mr. Hardy's unmarried sister, lived with the family most of the time and felt it necessary, since Mrs. Hardy was so easygoing, to keep the male members of the family in line. At present, Mrs. Hardy was away on a visit to the home of a girlhood friend in a near-by town.

Aunt Gertrude was a person with decided opinions, and right now she was wrought up about the plight of their widowed cousin Ruth. Ruth Hardy was having a hard time running her late husband's ranch because of a mysterious situation which had developed.

"If you don't go out there soon," said Aunt Gertrude, "I'm going myself!"

"I'll take care of Cousin Ruth in a few days," Mr. Hardy replied. "Sit down, Gertrude, and hear about this new case of ours."

"I'll not listen to a word of it," she said emphatically, "with poor Cousin Ruth out there alone with a lot of dishonest ranch hands, who'll likely murder her any minute!"

"I don't believe it's that bad," Mr. Hardy said soothingly. "But, anyhow, I'll go out and see Cousin Ruth within a week. Is that all right?"

"Well, see that it's soon," Aunt Gertrude spluttered. "And don't you boys get your father involved in one of your cases either, so he can't leave!"

With that Miss Hardy popped out of the room as quickly as she had entered. Frank and Joe grinned.

"Guess you got your orders, Dad," Joe remarked.

"Don't know as I blame her for worrying," Mr. Hardy said. "Cousin Ruth is in a tight spot, and I really should get out there and help her."

Secretly, Frank and Joe wished they might accompany their father to Ruth Hardy's ranch in New Mexico, but he had not suggested that they go along. Though they already had planned a camping trip with their stout, good-natured friend, Chet Morton, the boys would gladly have postponed it in favor of the trip out West.

"Dad," Frank said, "how about my taking this piece of strap to a laboratory for analysis? Perhaps we can find out what sort of person wore it?"

"Good idea," his father agreed.

It was too late that day to carry out Frank's suggestion, but early next morning Frank and Joe took the strap to a chemist in Bayport. He knew the boys well, and promised to have the analysis for them in twenty-four hours.

Frank and Joe hopped into their car and started home. As they rode along a residential street on the outskirts of town, a stop light flashed on, and Frank brought their car to a halt. At the near corner they noticed two men in conversation·

As the boys waited for the light to turn, one of the men on the sidewalk walked away. A moment later the second man suddenly slumped to the sidewalk. The other stranger turned and ran back. He bent over the stricken man briefly, then propped him up against a fire hydrant and hurried off again.

"Well, what do you know about that?" Frank remarked. "The fellow may be ill. We'd better help him."

The boys jumped out of the car and helped the man to his feet. As they did, he shook himself vigorously.

"Hey, let me alone!" he ordered. "What are you holding me for?"

"You collapsed," Frank told him. "Your friend didn't wait. How do you feel?"

"My friend?" the man asked.

"The one you were talking to," Joe said.

"He wasn't my friend," the man said as if irritated by the suggestion. "He just asked me for a light and . . . "

Suddenly the man felt his hip pocket and looked startled. Then he grabbed Frank and Joe and bellowed.

"Help! Help! I've been robbed! Arrest these boys!"

CHAPTER III

The Telltale Timepiece

"LET go!" Frank demanded. "We didn't take anything of yours."

"Then where's my wallet?" the man shouted. "It's got two hundred and fifty dollars in it!"

Suddenly the answer dawned on the boys. Right before their eyes they had witnessed one of the mysterious robberies which their father had been commissioned to solve!

"I'll go after the thief, Joe," Frank volunteered.

In a flash he was in the car, down the street, and out of sight, following the course taken by the suspect. Meanwhile, Joe got the full story from the victim.

"The fellow stopped me and asked for a light," he said. "I didn't have a match, so he went on. Then I passed out."

"That's where we came in," Joe said. "My

brother and I thought you had been taken ill. Ever see the thief before?"

"No." The man, now fully recovered, said he was tough-looking and rough-mannered.

Just then Frank pulled up to the curb. He stepped out of the car, followed by a policeman.

"The thief got away," the boy reported. "I spotted him three blocks from here, but he ducked into an alley."

"I saw Frank here lookin' for somebody," the policeman put in.

"By the way," said Joe, addressing the man, "this policeman can vouch for us."

"Sure can." The patrolman smiled. "These are the Hardy boys. Every cop on the force knows 'em. They're a couple of good detectives like their dad."

Quickly the victim of the robbery related to the officer what had happened. Then the four got into the Hardy car and drove to the police station, where the man made out a complete report. The boys left him there and went home.

They reported their new findings to Mr. Hardy. Then, since the chemist's report would not be ready till the following morning, the brothers spent the afternoon in the spacious room above their garage going over their camping equipment for the trip with Chet Morton. Joe unrolled a tent, counting all the pegs to be sure none were missing.

"Got your fly rod in shape?" Joe asked.

"It's right here," Frank added, drawing a sleek bamboo pole from a brown case. He fitted the three pieces together and attached the reel. "Sure is a beauty," he commented. "Ought to snag a couple of flat rainbows with it."

Just then Joe motioned toward a saddle which hung from a peg on the wall.

"What does this remind you of, Frank?" he asked.

"The time we went out West hunting for old Jad Wilson's missing gold. He sent us this saddle in appreciation."

"And it reminds me," said Joe, "of the trip to Cousin Ruth's ranch, which we'd like to make."

Joe took the saddle off its resting place and stroked the leather fondly. It was a big Western saddle— the kind one can ride in all day without tiring. Joe grasped the horn. A cowboy's rope, snubbed on this pinnacle, could pull any cow off its pins!

The boys were expert riders. For this reason, both were disappointed not to be going out West and riding range.

"We'll go sometime," Frank consoled his brother. "Right now we have a mystery to solve, and when that's finished we'll take a little trip of our own."

After breakfast the next day the telephone in the Hardy home rang. Frank answered, spoke a few words, and hung up.

"It's the chem lab," he said to Joe. "They've completed the analysis of the watch strap."

"Let's go!" cried his brother eagerly. "I want to get going on that mystery." He ran into the kitchen and flipped the car keys off a hook near the back door. "I'll meet you in front."

Joe guided the coupé out of the long driveway. Frank stepped into it at the curb, and the boys hurried to the laboratory. When they reached the place, the chemist greeted them with a smile.

"You boys just get back from Yellowstone Park?" he asked.

The brothers exchanged puzzled glances. "No," Frank said. "What makes you ask that?"

"Your interest in Indians," the scientist said.

"Indians?" Joe asked.

"Yes," the chemist replied. "I gather from the leather strap you brought in yesterday that you two are knee-deep in a case involving Indians."

"You've got me," said Frank, looking puzzled.

The chemist held up the watch strap in his hand.

"This strap," he began, like a professor lecturing a class, "has been worn by an Indian."

"How can you tell?" Joe asked.

"Simple enough. By the chemical properties of the perspiration it absorbed."

"Do you mean Indians have a different scent from white people?" Frank asked in surprise. "Say,

I've heard that all races don't smell alike, but I thought that was only a story."

"No, it's true," replied the chemist. "Every race has its own peculiar scent. That of the American Indian, like the odor of other races, has oftentimes been remarked upon."

"What's different about it?" Joe grinned. "Just so next time I'll know an Indian when I meet him in a breeze."

"Good question." The scientist laughed, tapping his pencil on the strap as if to emphasize his point.

"Travelers and explorers say the scent of American Indians is very agreeable. Seems to resemble the faint odor of cooking hominy. It doesn't have the heavy animal or musky smell that those of some other races have."

"I wonder why that is?" Frank asked.

"Perhaps," continued the chemist, "it's because the Indians have feebly developed scent glands."

"Do Indians think we smell different to them?" Joe put in. "Kind of musky?"

"Unfortunately, yes." The chemist smiled. "And what's more," he went on, "Indians say that they can tell a half-breed among them simply by the odor!"

"Well," Frank said with a long sigh, "so the watch strap belonged to an Indian."

The chemist smiled at the Hardys. "Does that help you?" he asked.

"Sure does," Frank said. "Now we've got to be on the lookout for Indians."

With that the brothers paid the chemist's fee and departed in their car.

"Say," Joe exclaimed, "do you think that guy who hit Slow Mo could be an Indian?"

"Could be. Or maybe an Indian owns the mysterious car, if he doesn't."

"That silver tie clip you found, Frank—an Indian might have made it."

"We'll soon find out," said his brother, pulling the clip from his pocket.

Examining it, he declared it was hand-wrought and looked like silverwork he had seen on Indian-made jewelry.

"Where you going?" Joe asked suddenly as Frank took a street leading out of town.

"Straight to Slow Mo's."

As he drew up in front of the weather-beaten garage in Pleasantville, the boys saw its proprietor seated on a straight-backed chair tilted against the side of the building. Upon seeing the Hardys, he sat forward.

"Did you solve the mystery?" he asked, showing a slight bit of excitement.

"No," Frank said.

"I didn't think you would," said Slow Mo and settled back again.

"We came to ask you some questions," Frank said. "Those people who left the car here, did they look like Indians?"

"Injuns?" Slow Mo pondered. "The man, he didn't look like one, but the woman—I never thought of that."

Slow Mo rolled his eyes skyward in deep meditation. "The woman," he continued slowly, "she could have been an Indian. Had straight black hair."

"What about the color of her skin?" Joe put in.

"Let's see. Yes, 'twas kinda dark," he replied.

The boys thanked the garage owner for his help and headed back toward Bayport. If Slow Mo's memory served him correctly, they had a good clue.

"But what I can't understand," Joe said, "is, if Indians are involved in the case at Slow Mo's, how it ties in with the crime wave in Bayport."

"Dad didn't say anything about Indians being involved in the thefts," Frank added, "but maybe they are."

"If that woman with the man who left the car at Slow Mo's is around here," Joe reasoned, "it shouldn't be hard to spot her."

"How about looking for her right now?" Frank said with determination.

The two boys drove up and down the streets of each town they came to but had no luck.

"People must think we're batty, looking at all the women," Joe said, grinning.

"It's in the line of duty," Frank laughed.

After they had combed the streets of Bayport, they finally gave up.

"Now what?" Frank asked.

"I've got it," Joe exclaimed, as if he had guessed the jack-pot question. "Let's look for the watch that went with the strap! It may still have the other piece of the strap attached."

"That's a long shot, but we can try," his brother said.

The boys stopped briefly for a bite to eat, then continued their search. First they went to all the jewelry repair shops in town.

"Got a watch with a broken strap to fit this piece?" Frank asked in place after place. Always the answer was no.

"Let's try secondhand shops," Joe suggested.

After canvassing half a dozen places and looking at scores of timepieces, they gave up. None had a broken strap to match the one they had found in the mysterious car.

"Only one kind of shop left," Joe sighed. "The pawnshops."

"Right. Let's try that one down there."

Frank and Joe gazed into the window of Maxby's three-ball, dingy store. It displayed pawned cameras, knives, and watches.

"I'll know enough about this to go into the hock and repair business myself," Joe said as they entered the shop.

"Got a watch with a broken strap to match this band?" Frank tossed the routine question.

"Think I have."

The answer shocked the boys into alert attention.

"Let's see it," Joe exclaimed.

The pawnbroker went to the back of the store and came out with a man's wrist watch. Part of the leather strap that flopped from it matched the piece Frank held in his hand!

"We've found it!" Joe exulted.

Frank said nothing. As the shopkeeper looked on curiously, he examined the watch. Holding it close to the light of the store window, he uttered a sharp exclamation.

"What's the matter?" Joe asked.

"Look, Joe!" Frank cried, pointing.

Across the top, cleverly etched into the design around the face of the timepiece, was a crooked arrow!

CHAPTER IV

An Alarming Message

IN AMAZEMENT Frank and Joe studied the sweeping
S crook of the arrow.

"What did you find?" asked the pawnbroker.
"An heirloom?"

"No," answered Frank, "just an old watch we've
been hunting for. Where did you get this?"

"I'll look," the man answered, thumbing through
a worn ledger. "Let's see."

Each day's transactions were listed on a separate
page of the book. The shopkeeper went back day
after day until he came to a page bearing the same
date as the day the black sedan had been left in
Slow Mo's garage.

"Here it is," he said. "This watch was pawned
by Annie Smith, 66 Grove Terrace."

"Did she look like an Indian?" Joe asked.

"She didn't look like an Indian to me," replied
the man, raising his eyebrows. Then he asked
nervously, "This isn't—er—a stolen watch, is it?"

Frank told the man he thought not. Then, thanking him for his trouble, he and Joe hastily left the store.

"Let's get to 66 Grove Terrace quick!" Frank said. "I'd like to meet this Annie Smith."

"Maybe you won't after you see her," Joe quipped, as he took the wheel and headed for Grove Terrace on the outskirts of Bayport.

"A pretty good street," Frank said. "Doesn't sound like a place where anybody poor would live."

"Never can tell," Joe remarked. "Maybe Annie Smith is a maid."

Soon he turned off the main thoroughfare onto a little street bearing the sign *Grove Terrace*.

Frank spotted the even numbers on the left side as they drove slowly down the road.

"Here's 50," Frank said. "And 62," he added as the coupé crept along. Suddenly he exclaimed, "Joe, *there isn't any 66!*"

The lot where No. 66 should have been was as vacant as the look on the boy's face. A tangle of small trees and sumac grew up through the heavy weeds.

"A phony address," Frank said.

Joe turned the car around and went back to the business section.

"I'm going into that pawnshop again and ask that guy some more questions," he declared.

"Not now," Frank said as they pulled up. "He's closed. Besides, Aunt Gertrude has supper ready, and we'd better not keep her waiting! We'll come back here in the morning."

Joe could hardly wait to finish his breakfast the next day, so eager was he to rush off. When Aunt Gertrude objected, he said:

"But this is a hot tip!"

"Makes no difference," his aunt replied. "First your father races down and eats nothing at all. Then you come along and want to leave this good food. Well, you're not going to. It's highway robbery what the stores charge, and bacon and eggs—Oh!"

Something in the kitchen was burning. Frank and Joe grinned as their aunt flew off. Scorched toast had ended the tirade!

Half an hour later the brothers drove up to the pawnshop. The proprietor was surprised to see them.

"Want to look at another watch?" he asked.

"No," said Frank as the man dangled a gold time-piece in front of him. "I want to find out who Annie Smith is."

"I gave you her address," the pawnbroker said.

"It's a fake," Joe interjected. "There isn't even a house at No. 66."

"No fault of mine," the man said in self-defense.

"We know that," Frank replied politely. "But we've got to find this Annie Smith. Perhaps you can help by giving us a description of her."

"What's wrong? She owe you money?"

"No." Frank laughed. "There's another reason. Now tell me. What does Annie Smith look like?"

The man hesitated a moment. Could he be covering up, the boys wondered. Was Annie Smith a pal of his in some crooked deal? As the boys pondered this question, the pawnbroker began slowly:

"Well, this Annie is a—whatcha call it—a character."

"You mean she's sort of queer?" Joe asked.

"Yeah, kinda queer, you might say. She comes around once in a while and pawns things."

Suddenly the pawnbroker grabbed Frank's arm.

"Hey, look!" he shouted. "There she goes now!"

Frank and Joe whirled around to catch a fleeting glimpse of a woman passing the dingy shopwindow. When the boys rushed out, she was only a few paces down the street. They caught up to her, and Frank, a trifle embarrassed, said:

"Beg your pardon, Miss Smith. There's something we'd like to ask you."

The woman, startled by the boys' sudden approach, looked at them with wild eyes. Her face was neither young nor old. She wore a slovenly dress, and her hair was untidy, hanging in wisps over her face.

"Sorry we frightened you," Joe apologized.

"What d' you want?" she asked.

"We'd like to know where you got the wrist watch you pawned a couple of months ago at Maxby's," Frank said.

"Me? I didn't pawn no watch," the woman replied. "What's it to you, anyway?"

"Then you did pawn a watch?" Joe queried.

"No."

"The records show you did," Frank said quietly. "You'd better tell us the truth."

"I won't tell anybody nuthin'," the woman said defiantly. "Now go away and don't bother me."

As Annie Smith started to push past the boys, Frank said:

"Well, Fenton Hardy might like to ask you a few questions if you don't tell us."

The name worked like magic. "Fenton Hardy?" Annie Smith repeated. "Oh, no. Please. I don't want to see no detectives!" Then she added nervously, "I'll tell you boys where I got the watch. I found it."

"Where?" Joe asked.

"Right in front of Al's Tobacco Shop."

With that Annie turned on her heel and hurried down the street.

"What do you make of it?" Joe asked.

"I think she's telling the truth," Frank said.

"She might be mixed up with some of that crooked arrow mob," Joe ventured. "Did you see how she jumped at the mention of Dad's name?"

"I have an idea," Frank put in. "Let's take a run over to the police station and check on her."

Shortly afterward the brothers walked into the office of Police Chief Collig. The officer pulled himself up in his chair until one of his chins rested comfortably on the other.

"Hello, boys," he said with dignity. "What can I do for you this time? Got another holdup to report?"

"We'd like to find out something about Annie Smith," Frank said.

"That's easy," the chief replied. "Nothing particularly wrong with Annie except she's got the wanderlust."

"Is she mixed up with any gang?" Joe queried.

"Naw," the chief said with a flourish of his hand. "Annie's just a harmless vagrant. Likes to pawn things she finds on the street. Once she found a necklace and got a tidy reward when she turned it in. She's harmless."

"Well, that seems to give Annie a clean bill of

health," Joe said, as the boys left the station house.

"But she did add a couple of clues to the case," Frank remarked.

"That's right," Joe agreed. "Since she pawned the watch on the same day the mystery car was left in Slow Mo's garage, the owner must have had business in Bayport."

"Maybe in Al's Tobacco Shop," Frank said. "Some of the victims of holdups said the men who stopped them asked for lights. Perhaps they trade at Al's."

"Al might even be mixed up with the gang," Joe ventured.

"He might even own another watch with a crooked arrow on it!" Frank added. "It's worth finding out."

The boys went to the tawdry little store, located in the water-front district of Bayport. A couple of rough-looking characters lounged outside.

"Here's where we get tough," Joe said, grinning.

As the boys strode into the dimly lighted store, Frank said to the man behind the counter, "Got any Baby Lu candy bars?"

The man, squat and beady-eyed, with a flattened nose, snorted and said, "Candy bars? This ain't no candy store. This is a respectable tobacco shop."

"I was just kiddin'," said Joe. "Are you Al?"

"Yeah."

"Gimme a pack of butts."

Al looked at the boys suspiciously.

"Hey, what are you kids snoopin' around here for?" he asked gruffly. "I don't sell nuthin' to minors."

"Okay," Joe said, taking in the layout of the dirty store in swift glances. "We'll go somewhere else."

"Got the time?" Frank asked suddenly, leaning over the counter to glance at the man's wrist watch.

Al obligingly held his hand toward the youth. The watch had a plain face, unadorned by any sort of doodads. There was no arrow, crooked or otherwise, etched on it.

"If you can read," Al said sarcastically, "you can see it's ten o'clock. Time for fresh kids to scram." Then he added menacingly, "Now get goin'!"

Frank and Joe left the place, walked down the street to where their car was parked, and drove toward home.

"I don't like him," Joe said. "I've got a hunch he winks at the law plenty."

"He'll bear watching," Frank agreed.

Disappointed that nothing had come of their clue, the boys decided to try finding their father and discussing the case with him. Frank parked the coupé in front of the Hardy house. They jumped out and entered the front door.

"I hope Dad's here," Joe said, walking instinctively toward the telephone table, where the Hardys always left notes to other members of the family. "Hey, what's this!" he exclaimed. "Mother's writing."

"She must be back from her trip," Frank said. "What did she say?"

The boys gazed at the memo pad, then gasped. On it, in a hurried hand, was a message that stunned Frank and Joe:

"Father in Bayport General Hospital. Shot. Come at once."

CHAPTER V

Heading Out West

"DAD shot!" Joe exclaimed.

The brothers stared at the note. There was no mistaking the ominous news.

"This is mother's handwriting, all right," Frank declared. "Aunt Gertrude's not here, either. Come on, Joe, we'd better hurry to the hospital!"

They raced outside and sped toward the hospital as fast as the law would permit. The usually ebullient Joe sat in worried silence as his brother stopped for one traffic light after another.

Finally the boys drove up in front of a large building on which the name *Bayport General Hospital* was carved in gleaming marble. They dashed up to the information desk.

"We're Mr. Fenton Hardy's sons," Frank said to the woman behind the desk. "We'd like to see him right away."

The woman looked in her files, telephoned the third floor of the surgical wing, then said:

"You may see him a few moments, Room 328."

Their footsteps echoed hollowly as they approached the door of the room. Joe gripped his brother's arm as they entered. A screen concealed the patient and the boys heard the low tone of conversation behind it. Together they stepped around the screen, and stood beside the bed.

In it lay Fenton Hardy, pale and restless. His eyes were closed and he was breathing deeply. Standing beside him were his wife, Aunt Gertrude, a young doctor, and a nurse.

"What happened?" Frank asked in a hoarse whisper. Mrs. Hardy put a finger to her lips and motioned for the boys to come closer.

"Mr. Hardy isn't quite out of the anesthetic yet," the doctor said. "Bad wound in his leg."

The boys could hardly restrain themselves. "Is it s-serious?" Joe asked.

"Serious," replied the doctor quietly, "but not critical. Your father will pull out of it soon, provided no complications set in."

Mrs. Hardy took each of her sons by the arm and guided them into the corridor, where they could talk without disturbing the wounded man.

"Tell us about it," Frank pleaded.

"How many bullets hit Dad?" Joe put in, his voice trembling.

"He wasn't shot by a gun," Mrs. Hardy said, putting a comforting hand around Joe's shoulder.

"He wasn't?" Frank asked incredulously.

"No," their mother replied. "He was . . . "

"Mrs. Hardy!" It was the doctor's voice. She hurried back into the room. "Your husband wants to see his sons," the physician said.

Fenton Hardy, struggling through the limbo between consciousness and unconsciousness, had heard the far-off voices of his boys and had roused sufficiently to call them weakly. Now he was completely out of the anesthetic, and had opened his eyes.

"Dad!" Frank whispered, taking the open hand extended toward him.

Joe pressed close to his brother. "How are you, Dad?"

"I'm all right," Mr. Hardy said, forcing a smile. "I'll be up and out of here in no time."

"Mother said you weren't shot by a gun," Frank said. "What did hit you?"

Fenton Hardy turned his head with effort, to get a better look at his sons.

"An arrow," he said.

"It hit him high in the left leg," the physician said. "A nasty wound, deep to the bone."

Aunt Gertrude continued the story, giving her brother a chance to rest.

"Your father said he was investigating a vacant house on the outskirts of town, which he thought some of the Bayport thieves were using as a hide-out."

"Were they inside?" Joe asked.

"No," continued their aunt. "The place was empty, but just after your father left the house, an arrow came from behind and hit him."

Mr. Hardy carried on. "Then I staggered to the road for help."

"Did you see the guy who shot you?" Joe asked.

"No, son," he replied. "He must have been waiting in the bushes behind the house."

After pausing a moment, the detective continued, "This means I can't go to Cousin Ruth's. Would you boys like to take my place?"

Frank and Joe looked at each other, then nodded in unison.

"I know Chet will be disappointed when you postpone your camping trip," Mr. Hardy added, "but— say, why don't you take Chet along?"

The physician interrupted, "That's all for now, please. Mr. Hardy must rest."

"You boys go along with Aunt Gertrude," Mrs. Hardy said. "I'll not leave your father until he's better!"

Frank and Joe kissed their mother and said good-bye to their father. Then they left with Miss Hardy.

At the hospital entrance the three ran into Sam Radley, Mr. Hardy's operative, who was hurrying into the building.

"How's Mr. Hardy?" he asked breathlessly. "I just learned he's here."

Frank told the tall, worried investigator all he knew of the attack. Sam frowned when he heard about the arrow.

"It's most unusual," he remarked.

"Why the dickens would anybody shoot him with an arrow?" Joe asked.

"Probably," Sam replied, "to escape detection. It'll be harder to trace an arrow than a bullet. Where's the arrow?"

"At the police station," Aunt Gertrude said. "My brother ordered it sent there immediately."

"We'd better take a look at it," Sam suggested.

The investigator took Aunt Gertrude in his car, while the boys drove their coupé to the police station. Alone in the car, Frank said to Joe:

"Does something click about this whole case?"

"Yes," Joe replied slowly. "The arrow!"

"That's it," Frank said. "First Dad picked up the words 'crooked arrow' on his recorder. Then we found the crooked arrow on the watch and tie clasp."

"And now Dad is shot with an arrow by an unknown archer." Joe put in.

"It all seems to add up," Frank reasoned. "But to what? One thing's clear. Some crook or crooks are afraid of Dad."

The two cars arrived at the station house about the same time. Aunt Gertrude, Sam, and the boys were ushered into the office of Chief Collig. He sat at his desk examining an arrow.

"Hello, boys," he said. "Awfully sorry to hear what happened to your father."

"Any clues to the assailant?" Frank asked.

"None at all. My men searched the place and found a trampled spot in the weeds, where the culprit apparently drew a sight on your father, but nothing else."

"See that you find the man!" Aunt Gertrude blurted out with indignation. "The idea of anybody shooting my brother! And with an arrow, no less. What's happened to police protection in Bayport?"

"We've tried our—"

"Your best isn't good enough!" Aunt Gertrude interrupted the chief. "I'll find that scoundrel myself and punish him!"

As Sam Radley looked on with approval, Frank asked, "May I see the arrow, chief?"

Collig handed him a short, thick shaft with a sharp steel tip. On the end, near the nock, were three white feathers.

"This could kill a man," Frank said seriously, turning the arrow in his fingers.

"Sure could," Chief Collig agreed. "Your father was lucky."

"Look at those feathers," Joe observed. "They're all the same color."

"Aren't they supposed to be?" Aunt Gertrude spoke up.

"Two of the feathers on an arrow," Joe explained, "are usually the same color, such as red. The other, known as the cock feather, stands at right angles to the nock, and is of a different color."

"Then an expert archer must have shot this arrow," Frank added. "He didn't need a colored feather to show him which was the cock feather."

"Right," Sam said. "And he didn't mean to kill your father; just incapacitate him. Well, we've got to look for an expert archer."

"Then we'll start on the Indians in town," Frank suggested, giving Joe a significant glance.

"We have only four of 'em in Bayport," Chief Collig told the boys. "And they're all honest, so far as I know."

Nevertheless, Frank and Joe got the names of the Indians. They might be honest, but they might have some dishonest relative visiting them who would bear investigating!

After bidding Sam good-bye and taking Aunt Gertrude home, the boys started out to question the four local Indians in the factory section of town. All were skilled at trades and had worked well for their employers, the Hardys learned. None had visitors and none had handled a bow in his life. They emphatically denied any knowledge of the shooting of Mr. Hardy.

"Looks as if Bayport's Indians are innocent, all right," Frank said. "That makes it harder to solve this new mystery."

"And we haven't much time left to find the archer," Joe reminded his brother, "if we're going to Cousin Ruth's."

"We'd better tell Chet of the change in our plans," Frank said. "Think he'll go out West with us?"

Joe grinned. "We'll say Cousin Ruth has a good chuck wagon!"

Chet Morton, chubby, food-loving friend of the Hardy boys, lived on a farm a short distance outside Bayport. When they arrived, Frank pulled up alongside the porch of the rambling Morton home. Iola Morton, Chet's sister, was on the porch.

"Hello, Iola," shouted Joe, blushing a little. He was rather fond of Iola. "Where's Chet?"

"Behind the barn," the girl replied.

Frank parked in front of the barn and the boys made their way to the back. Suddenly they spied their stocky friend Chet, crouching like a football lineman. Rushing at him was a big man, his arms outstretched.

Then, faster than the eye could follow, he grabbed Chet and flipped him into the air!

CHAPTER VI

Poisoned Arrowhead

CHET landed on the ground with a thud. Frank and Joe rushed to his aid. As the elder brother quickly knelt beside his fallen friend, Chet looked up and said casually:

"Hi, Frank! What did you think of that flip-flop?"

As Chet rose to his feet and called to the young man who had tossed him, the Hardys looked puzzled.

"Come here, Russ." He grinned. "I want you to meet two friends of mine."

A pleasant-looking fellow greeted them. He had a slender waist and broad shoulders, which looked all the sturdier because of his crew haircut.

"This is Russ Griggs," Chet said as the young man shook hands with Joe and Frank. "He's teaching me judo."

"Chet's a pretty good pupil," Russ said, tugging at his belt. "But he's quite a load to toss over your shoulder."

"Russ is an ex-Marine," Chet went on proudly. "He learned all this stuff when he was in the Orient."

"Gosh," Joe said, "we thought you were murdering Chet!"

"Not quite as bad as that." Russ laughed. "We were just working on a movement against the back."

Frank and Joe exchanged glances. What was Chet up to now? They asked him.

"Well," Chet said, grinning, "I'm always getting into some kind of jam helping you fellows solve a mystery. I figure Russ can teach me something useful."

"Not a bad idea," Joe chimed in. "Might be good for us too, eh, Frank?"

"We know a couple of judo holds already," Frank said, "but that last one you used on Chet was a honey!"

"It's easy enough, if you're fast," Russ told them. "Here, I'll show you how it goes."

As Frank stepped forward, the ex-Marine showed him the fundamentals of the hold, taking each step slowly.

"Now, try it on me," he said.

Hardly were the words out of his mouth when

the husky Russ went zooming through the air like a rocket bomb. Frank was an apt student.

"Hey!" Russ shouted. "I didn't expect you to move that fast!"

The boys laughed and the judo expert showed them a variety of other holds.

"Now," Chet said as perspiration trickled off his chin, "bring on the villain!"

After the young man had left, Frank and Joe quickly told Chet about the attack on their father.

"Shot by an arrow!" Chet exclaimed in amazement, and added, "Gosh, I'm sure sorry to hear he got hurt."

"We'll have to postpone our camping trip," Joe told him.

"I can understand that," Chet said sympathetically. "You want to be near your dad."

"It's for another reason," Frank put in. "He wants us to go to New Mexico. Our cousin Ruth Hardy, who owns the Crowhead Ranch out there, is having a lot of trouble."

"How'd you like to come with us, Chet?" Joe burst out suddenly.

"Yippee!" Chet exclaimed. "Slap my chaps and call me cowboy! I'll get my stuff together right away—blankets and frying pan, and a side of bacon."

"Wait a minute." Frank laughed. Then he

winked at Joe. "It'll have to be short rations for you, Chet. Have to slim down for hard riding on the range."

"Frank's right," Joe took up the needling. "A horse would break his back toting you around!"

"Aw, quit your kidding," Chet pleaded.

Just then the voice of Iola sounded from the porch. "Refreshments are ready," she called.

Frank and Joe held Chet back for a moment. Then they dashed ahead of him to the porch.

"Oh, hello, Callie," Frank said, seeing another girl with Iola Morton.

Callie Shaw was Iola's best friend and, so far as Frank Hardy was concerned, was as nice a girl as any fellow would like to know.

"Hi, boys!" Callie responded cheerfully. "Help yourself to lemonade and cakes."

"Take it easy now, Chet," Joe warned. "Remember, you're on a diet!"

"I'll start tomorrow," Chet said.

While they ate, Frank, Joe, and Chet talked and joked with the girls. Then the conversation turned to the mystery the Hardys had run into at Slow Mo's garage.

"I know you can find the answer," Callie said, looking at Frank. "You always do."

The telephone rang and Mrs. Morton answered it. "It's for you, Frank," she said.

Frank went inside, spoke a few words, and came back to the porch.

"It was Slow Mo," he told Joe. "He's dug up some new information and wants to see us."

"How'd he know you were here?" Chet asked.

"Aunt Gertrude told him where he'd probably find us," Frank said. "Hate to break up the party, but we ought to go."

The two girls and Chet walked out to the Hardy's car and waved as Frank and Joe went down the driveway and headed for Pleasantville. As they came to a stop in front of the old man's garage, Slow Mo ambled out to meet them.

"More funny business goin' on around here," he announced.

"What happened?"

"Some smart aleck tried to take that car last night," he replied. "But I fooled him."

"How?" Joe put in.

Slow Mo scratched his whiskers and grinned. "Well, he got in a window, but when he tried to open the garage doors my burglar alarm went off and scared him away!"

"Good for you!" Frank said. "When did you put the alarm in?"

"Oh, a long time ago," Slow Mo replied. He looked a little sheepish. "I never thought to turn it on 'til last night."

The boys went into the garage and looked around. The mystery car had been moved halfway across the floor, as if the intruder had taken it that far before stopping to get out and open the doors.

"Did you find any clues?" Frank queried.

"Nothin'," Slow Mo said, " 'cept the fellow must be a chicken farmer."

"What makes you think so?" Joe asked.

"He left a chicken feather on the seat of the car," he replied. "Here, take a look at it."

The man reached an oily hand into his pocket and drew out a white feather, now somewhat smudged.

"Brother!" Joe exclaimed. "What a clue!"

"A clue?" Slow Mo looked puzzled. "Never thought of that. 'Taint nothin' but a chicken feather to me."

Frank and Joe thanked Slow Mo for the information and headed back to Bayport.

"I think we have something here," Frank said as the boys hummed along the highway.

"This feather sure looks like the one on the arrow that wounded Dad."

After parking in front of the police station, the boys hurried inside. The chief was not there, but the sergeant in charge obligingly let them examine the arrow again. Frank compared the feathers.

"Look, Joe!" he said excitedly. "They match!"

"Then the guy who dropped this at Slow Mo's

may be the one who shot Dad," Joe exclaimed. "We've got to find him."

At the mention of Mr. Hardy, the sergeant pricked up his ears. "Too bad about him," he declared mournfully. "I know how you must feel."

"Too bad about what?" Frank said quickly.

"Haven't you heard?" the officer asked in surprise. "The arrow that shot your father was poisoned. If he should die—"

Without waiting for another word, the boys raced to their car and drove to the hospital in record time. When they reached their father's room, they found him very ill. Mrs. Hardy sat holding her husband's hand.

"Your father was poisoned by that arrow," she said to her sons, a sob in her voice. "The doctors are doing all they can to counteract the poison."

Mr. Hardy was too weak to speak, but he smiled faintly at the boys.

"You'd better go now," Mrs. Hardy said. "I'll phone the house if I need you."

Worried at this unexpected turn of events, the boys went downstairs. As they were about to step out the front door, the receptionist called to them.

"You're the Hardy boys, aren't you?"

When Frank nodded, she added, "Chief Collig just called. He wants to see you at police headquarters."

When the boys arrived there, the officer ushered them into the line-up room. Standing on a dais were three men. A bright light shone into their faces.

"We've had a dragnet out for the man who shot your father," the chief told the brothers. "My men rounded up these suspects today. I've questioned each one at length, but these fellows all have air-tight alibis, and they don't know a thing about archery. I was going to let them go, but I thought maybe you'd like to look at them and ask a few questions."

Frank asked the men if any of them traded at Slow Mo's garage in Pleasantville; also if any of them kept white chickens or turkeys. All said no.

"Sorry," Chief Collig said. "We'll round up some more men."

The brothers drove home. After Mrs. Hardy telephoned from the hospital that their father was somewhat improved, but that she was remaining there, the boys ate dinner and went to bed.

Next morning their mother telephoned that Mr. Hardy was much better, which buoyed the boys' spirits.

"Joe," said Frank, putting his arm around the younger boy's shoulder, "we'll have to take a new tack today to locate our crook. We got exactly no-where yesterday."

"You're right," Joe agreed. "Tell you what. Let's stop every stranger in town and ask what time it is. Perhaps we can spot another wrist watch with a crooked arrow."

Together the brothers drove to the busy downtown area and parked their car. Then they began the tedious task of asking the time of every man they saw who was not familiar to them. As the hours wore on, the answer was a polite "eleven-thirty," "one-fifteen," "three-forty-five." Still the boys persisted.

About four o'clock, Frank, across the street from where Joe was working, stopped a husky fellow, who wore a cap pulled low on his forehead. Instead of giving the boy the time, the man clasped his hand over his wrist watch and growled:

"Get out of my way!"

CHAPTER VII

An Amazing Discovery

FRANK stepped toward the man who had refused to let him see his wrist watch.

Suddenly the fellow cocked his left arm. A heavy fist flashed. Before Frank could move, the blow caught him flush on the point of the chin! Frank staggered backward against a building, stunned by the unexpected blow.

"Stop him!" Joe shouted, as the man dashed down the street.

But the people who had witnessed the scene merely stared, letting the stranger make a clean getaway.

"I'll catch him!" Joe gritted, racing across the street to his brother's side. "Meet you at the car," he told Frank, who by this time had recovered his equilibrium.

The man was a block ahead when Joe spotted him snaking among the pedestrians. But the boy, fired

by determination to nab Frank's attacker and perhaps find a new clue to the mystery of the crooked
arrow, doggedly sprinted after the man.

Joe gained yard after yard, leaving a trail of
gaping onlookers. Presently he found himself in a
section of the water front that seemed strangely
familiar. The man was running down the street
which claimed the dubious distinction of having Al's
Tobacco Shop on it!

Hearing Joe's footsteps close behind, the man
glanced over his shoulder and put on an extra spurt
of speed. A moment later he dashed into the tobacco shop.

When Joe ran through the doorway, his quarry
was leaning against the counter, puffing like a
locomotive.

"What's the idea of hitting my brother?" the boy
asked defiantly.

He clenched his fists in readiness, not wanting to
be caught off guard if the stranger should lunge at
him.

"Your—your brother's a wise guy," the man
wheezed. "Tried to look at my watch when I don't
even have one on."

Joe glanced at the man's wrists. There was no
watch. But the boy noted a section of slightly
untanned skin on his left arm as if a watch had been
worn recently.

"You had a watch on," Joe retorted. "What **did** you do with it?"

Al, who was standing behind the counter, looked at Joe. "That fresh kid again," he said menacingly. "You got an unhealthy interest in watches. Why don't you chase along home and keep out of trouble?"

Joe had all he could do to refrain from taking a punch at both men. But he knew that he would be no match for Al and the stranger.

"Okay," he said, and walked out.

But Joe had no intention of dropping the matter. The fact that the chase had led to the tobacco shop was too good a clue not to follow up.

Joe was eager to get back to his brother and tell him of this new angle. He trotted off to the place where they had parked their car. Frank was waiting.

"Find out anything, Joe?" he asked. "I thought maybe something had happened to you."

His brother quickly related what had taken place.

"We've got to investigate Al's place thoroughly," he said. "I have a feeling he's connected in some way with the Bayport crooks."

"It's a sure bet Al won't give us any information," Frank reasoned.

"How about Sam Radley?" suggested Joe. "Maybe he could case the place for us."

"Don't think so," Frank replied. "Sam's too busy trying to find Dad's assailant. Besides, if Al's mixed up with crooks, he's probably been told Sam is a detective."

"I've got it!" Joe exclaimed, snapping his fingers. "Chet can help us!"

"Good idea," Frank agreed. "Chet might go in and ask some questions. Al wouldn't suspect him. He looks too innocent."

In a few minutes the telephone rang at the Morton farm. Chet himself answered it.

"Hello, Frank," he said cheerfully. "All ready to start out West?"

"Not yet." Frank laughed. "First we want you to help us on a case."

"Oh, oh!" said Chet. "I knew this was coming!"

Frank quickly outlined what he wanted his friend to do. Chet did not sound too enthusiastic at the prospect.

"What's the matter?" Frank asked. "You aren't afraid, are you?"

"Those are pretty tough guys hanging around that part of town," Chet protested.

"You can handle 'em," Frank came back. "What about those judo lessons you're taking?"

"You bet," Chet burst out. "I'll throw 'em over my shoulder." Frank could imagine Chet swelling with pride on the other end of the line.

"Good," Frank replied. "See you tomorrow morning at ten at our house. We'd make it earlier, but we want to stop at the hospital to see Dad."

Chet arrived at the Hardy home a little late, and insisted upon a second breakfast before his visit to Al's Tobacco Shop.

"You're supposed to be reducing," Frank reminded him.

Chet grimaced. "I need energy if I have to fight any tough guys," he declared. "By the way, how's your father?"

"Much better," Frank replied. "He sure gave us a scare, though."

As the three boys started off a few minutes later, Frank outlined their plan of operation.

"Joe will keep an eye on the front door," he said. "I'll station myself in the delivery alley at the back of the place."

"What do I do?" Chet asked nervously.

"You go inside." Frank continued, "and see if you can spot anything resembling a crooked arrow; watch, tie clip, or other jewelry. Meanwhile, try to find out if Al sells anything to his regular customers besides tobacco."

"Maybe you'd better go in," Chet said, looking at Frank apprehensively, "while I stand at the back of the place."

"Why, Chet," Joe said, keeping a straight face,

"you know a lot more about judo than we do!"

"Oh, well, all right," Chet agreed finally. "But I've got a feeling I'm running right smack into trouble."

Frank parked the coupé a block from the scene, and the boys started work according to plan. Joe stood in the doorway of an old house almost directly across the street from the shop. Frank concealed himself behind three tall ash cans in the back of the store. Chet, screwing up his courage, entered the store. All had agreed to meet ten minutes later in a diner down the street.

But they did not have to wait that long. Frank heard the back screen door of Al's shop bang shut. Poking his head around one of the cans to get a better view, he saw a rough-looking man stop momentarily, look up and down, then quietly slip down the alley.

Hardly had the man departed when the sound of angry words and scuffling issued from the shop. Frank could hear Al growl in a low tone and Chet reply in a high-pitched voice.

"Leggo of me!" Chet cried. "If you don't, I'll— I'll—"

A crash followed and the screen door flew open. A blurred figure bounced into the alley, rolling nearly to the ash cans.

At first Frank had thought Chet, using his newly

learned judo, had tossed Al from the store. But the figure that struggled to its feet was not the shop owner!

"Chet!" Frank whispered, standing up from his hiding place. "What happened?"

"Tell you later," Chet puffed. "Let's get out of here!"

Frank led the way, with Chet limping behind. They made their way to the diner, where Joe was waiting. He told of having seen a man enter the store just before Chet did.

"That's right. Al was waiting on him when I stepped in. Called him Bearcat. They didn't notice me."

"Did you hear anything?" Frank asked quickly.

"The fellow said 'Got any arrows?' Chet related. "Al handed him something, but I didn't get a good look at what it was."

"Arrows!" Joe gasped. "Go on. What happened next?"

"Bearcat said, 'I'll be at Mike's,' and went out the back door," Chet replied. "Then Al saw me. When I said I wanted some cigars for my dad, he got mad and threw me out. Said I was a pest and a sneak and—well, I think he didn't like my coming in so suddenly. Guess I interrupted something that made Al sore."

"It's something to do with arrows, that's sure," Frank declared.

"Whatever arrows are, they're small," Chet said. "And where is Mike's?"

"I know!" Frank declared. "I saw it on the way here. It's a cheap restaurant two blocks down the water front; the place where Dad's recorder picked up the words 'crooked arrow.' "

"Let's go!" Joe exclaimed.

"No," Frank warned. "I'll go alone. Too many of us would arouse suspicion. But if I'm not back in fifteen minutes, come after me."

Joe and Chet agreed to stay at the diner until Frank completed his trip to Mike's. He strode down the street, determined to find the man he had seen in the alley behind Al's Tobacco Shop.

It was not long before the boy was standing in front of Mike's Place. Several rough-looking men walked in and out through the swinging doors.

"Guess I'd better act the part," Frank thought with a smile.

Taking off his necktie, he put it in his pocket and unbuttoned his collar. Then, trying to look as tough as Mike's clientele, he mussed up his hair.

Frank walked boldly into the restaurant. At first he could see almost nothing in the place, which was dimly lighted and filled with cigarette smoke that hung like a pall over the old-fashioned wooden tables.

As his eyes became accustomed to the gloom, Frank looked eagerly at the faces of the men in the place. None resembled the one he sought.

Disappointed, Frank worked his way toward the back of the restaurant. He spotted a booth at the extreme rear. In it sat Bearcat!

Frank slipped into the seat opposite him. The man hardly noticed the boy as he scanned the menu, written in pencil. When he finally glanced at Frank, the boy leaned forward.

"Say, Al ain't got no more arrows," he whispered. "How about lettin' me have one?"

The man's eyes narrowed suspiciously.

"You in the racket, too, eh?" he said. "Nuttin' like startin' when you're young."

He reached into his pocket and drew out a cigarette. Frank opened his wallet and laid a ten-dollar bill on the table. With no idea of its price, he was sure this would amply cover the cost. To his amazement the man gave him no change.

"Al sure is a gyp," whined Frank. "A guy can't get far with one Arrow."

"Ain't Al's fault," Bearcat replied.

"Thanks," Frank said, pocketing the cigarette and rising to leave.

Then he stopped short. Coming in the front door

was Al himself. As he headed for Frank's booth, the boy slipped out of it, concealing himself as best he could behind a barrellike waiter. Fortunately, Al's eyes took a few seconds to become accustomed to the dimness and he failed to notice Frank as he made for the door.

"Hey, you," the gruff voice of the cashier called. "Pay up!"

"I didn't eat anything," Frank objected.

"Oh, no? Say, kid, you pay or—"

Al had stopped to listen to the argument. Frank was fearful. He threw a dollar bill to the cashier, saying:

"Okay, but I'll come back and eat it out later."

With that Frank hurried into the street, half running toward the diner where Joe and Chet were waiting. In his hand he held the Arrow cigarette.

At last he knew what the mysterious thing was—a cigarette!

As the boy neared the diner, Frank turned the cigarette over in his fingers to take a quick look at it.

Suddenly he saw black spots before his eyes. His head swam, then he slumped to the sidewalk!

CHAPTER VIII

Arrow Charlie

"FRANK, Frank! What's the matter?" Joe bent over his brother, his face tense and worried.

"I . . . I . . . wh . . . where am I?" Frank asked, regaining consciousness.

"You're on the sidewalk," Joe replied. "When you didn't show up, we started looking for you and found you here."

With Joe's aid, Frank struggled to his feet. As his brain cleared, he told what had happened at Mike's Place.

"I was on my way back to meet you fellows," he said, "when I took a look at the cigarette and then . . . Hey, where is it?"

Frank suddenly gazed about him.

"This it?" Joe inquired, picking up a cigarette that had rolled into the gutter.

"Yes," Frank said. "Let's look it over carefully—but not here."

"Where, then?" Chet asked.

"At the police station," Frank replied.

The three drove quickly to headquarters. On the way, Frank related in detail what had happened in the restaurant and how he had paid ten dollars for the Arrow cigarette.

"I'm sure this cigarette put me to sleep," Frank reasoned. "And if it did, we may have the key to the Bayport robberies."

Joe was so excited he could hardly wait to tell Chief Collig the story.

"This is top secret," Frank said as the police officer greeted the trio.

The boy motioned for the doors to be closed. The chief obliged, stationing a subordinate outside.

"Don't let anybody in," he instructed the policeman, "until I've finished this conference with the Hardy boys."

Then he turned to the trio. "Have you located the man who shot your father?" he asked with quickening interest.

"No," Frank replied as spokesman for the boys. "But we've uncovered a clue that may solve the mysterious robberies around Bayport."

With that he pulled the cigarette from his pocket and laid it on the chief's desk.

"What's this, a joke?" Collig asked.

"It's no joke," Frank insisted. "This is a cigarette that can put you to sleep!"

"What?"

"That's what happened to me."

Frank hastily related the story of the scene in Al's Tobacco Shop, and concluded with his own adventure in the restaurant.

"I'll have this Arrow analyzed at once," declared Chief Collig. "Don't touch it. I'll get the head of our crime lab."

He pressed a button on his intercommunication system. A hollow voice answered.

"Send Creech in to see me," Collig ordered.

A few moments later a bald-headed man wearing tortoise-shell glasses entered the office.

"I want you to analyze a cigarette right away," the officer said.

"Okay, chief," he answered. "I'll have the report in a few minutes."

While Collig and the boys talked over the many aspects of the Bayport crime wave, in which one thief nicknamed Bearcat was involved, Creech went to work quickly in the laboratory. In ten minutes he returned holding a white sheet of cardboard in his hands. On it were the component parts of the Arrow cigarette.

"Here we are," he said. "This sure is a newfangled kind of cigarette. Where did you boys get it; in a toy novelty shop?"

"No, indeed."

The technician explained what he had found in the strange cigarette.

"There's genuine tobacco at both ends," he said, pointing to the shreds of tobacco leaf on the white cardboard. "But in the middle there's a queer gadget."

"What is it?" Joe asked quickly.

Creech held a little capsule between his fingers. It was about an inch long. At one end was a tiny stem.

"What the dickens is that?" Chief Collig thundered.

"Sort of a little bomb," the technician explained. "It could hold a liquid or a gas."

"What's the stem for?" Frank queried.

"That," Creech answered, "is a plunger. The end of the plunger was flush with one end of the cigarette."

"Would it release the stuff inside the capsule?" Joe asked.

"Right," came the reply. "Pressure on the plunger trips a spring inside the tiny vial to free whatever is in it."

"What was in the capsule?" Collig asked

"That I can't tell," Creech answered, "but I think it might have been some sort of gas." Then he smiled at the boys and added, "Is this gadget for a party prank?"

"No, sirree," Frank replied. "I think the chief knows what it is. If he wants to tell you, that's all right with me."

Creech glanced at the chief, whose furrowed brow indicated he was battling with a tough problem. He looked at the Hardys.

"You boys have done Bayport a great service," he said. Then he turned to Creech. "This cigarette," he said, "is being used by criminals to knock out their victims."

Immediately it dawned on the technician. "I get it!" he exclaimed. "The crook holds the cigarette near the intended victim and presses the plunger. Then the gas, or whatever it is, knocks the person out long enough to be robbed!"

"Exactly," Frank said. "When I pressed the plunger by accident, I saw spots before my eyes and keeled over."

"This must be kept secret," Collig said. "Aside from telling Mr. Hardy and Sam Radley, you boys must keep this quiet."

As the three agreed, Frank added, "Wonder what kind of gas the crooks use? It had no lasting effect on me. I feel fine now."

Again Collig pressed a button on his desk. "Al's shop will be raided at once," he told the boys, as the door opened and a sergeant entered. "Want to come along?"

"You bet! And we'll have to hurry. Bearcat's probably tipped off Al by now," Frank said.

The police, led by the chief and the three boys, speeded to the shop. Their sirens were muted, so as not to advertise their arrival to Al or any of his confederates.

Chief Collig's aide deftly steered the big black police sedan through the downtown traffic and headed for the water front. Then, with tires and breaks squealing, it pulled up in front of Al's. In a moment two other carloads of police joined them.

Frank and Joe were told to stay in the rear, in case there should be trouble. Chet lingered at the sidewalk, fascinated by the squad of bluecoats who issued from the police cars.

"Nobody's here!" exclaimed Collig in the lead.

"Hey, smells like something's burning," Frank cried out, joining him.

He ran to the back door and looked into the alley, just in time to see Al hotfooting it away. A smoldering package lay by the door.

"Stop!" Frank shouted at him.

As he called, two policemen appeared at the end of the alley, cutting off the man's escape. They collared Al at once and brought him to Chief Collig.

Frank stamped out the fire in the package, most of which had been reduced to black char.

"Look here, chief!" Frank exclaimed, kicking what was left to one side and opening a cigarette at arm's length. "They're Arrows!"

"What does this mean?" Chief Collig growled, addressing the surly Al.

"I ain't done nuthin'" came the reply. "Just burned some stale cigarettes."

Joe took one of them in his fingers. It had been burned halfway through. Nothing was left but half the capsule, which smoldered with a peculiar odor.

"The capsule burns!" he cried out. "It's made of some sort of plastic!"

"That's probably why we haven't found any evidence before," Collig said. "The thieves burn up the cigarettes and leave no evidence."

He ordered handcuffs slipped on Al. "Come on!" he said. "You've got a lot of explaining to do at headquarters."

"I ain't explainin' a thing," the man declared stubbornly.

While this was going on in the alley, other police officers had searched the store. They had found nothing but a meager stock of popular brands of tobacco. He had burned all the telltale evidence!

"We'll take this man in my car," said Collig.

When the Hardys arrived at the station, they bade the chief good-bye, took Chet to a bus that stopped at his farm, and then hurried to the hospital.

Mr. Hardy, who was improving slowly, listened with admiration to his sons' account of the discovery of the Arrow cigarettes.

"There's one thing we must do soon," he said.

"I think I know what you mean," Frank put in to keep his father from overexerting himself. "Rout out all the Arrow cigarettes in this area, and see if we can pick up any clues to what is used or where the cigarettes come from."

"Right." Mr. Hardy smiled. "Without the loaded cigarettes, the crooks won't be able to commit such bold robberies." Then he added, "Meanwhile, suppose you boys get ready to go to Cousin Ruth's. You ought to make reservations on the train before the end of the week."

Next morning, Frank and Joe got in touch with Sam Radley, and the three set out to locate more Arrow cigarettes. While the local police undertook to do the job in Bayport, Sam and the boys drove to near-by towns, which also had experienced an outbreak of holdups.

They stopped in all sorts of shops where cigarettes might be sold, asking the same question:

"Have you any Arrows? Al sent us to get some."

Time after time the boys, working apart from

Sam, were met by vacant stares and, "Don't know what you're talking about!"

But in Green Point, a village near Pleasantville, a tobacco shopman replied, "Al sent you?"

"Yep," Frank answered, his pulse quickening.

"Got anything to show?" the man asked.

"Crooked arrow!" Joe said, hoping that might be the password.

"Good enough for me," came the reply.

With that the man gave the boys two cigarettes, for which they paid twenty dollars. The shopkeeper leaned close to the boys.

"Tell Al those are my last two," he whispered. "Have him send Arrow Charlie around with a new lot as soon as he gets back from Mexico."

Frank and Joe looked as casual as they could, though their pulses were racing.

"Oh, sure," Frank said. "Arrow Charlie. Say, did he get that name from selling Arrows or is he a good archer? We never heard."

The man smiled crookedly. "You boys ought to know," he said. "A fellow in Bayport got shot by an arrow the other day!"

That was enough for the Hardys. They hurried to their car and whizzed back toward the city to report the Green Point tobacconist and turn over the cigarettes for analysis.

As they hummed down the road which ran past

the Morton farm, they saw Chet on the porch. When they tooted their horn, he waved frantically. Frank jammed on the brake and Chet puffed up to them, a worried look on his face.

"Your mother phoned here a few minutes ago, wanting to get hold of you," he panted.

"What's up?" Joe asked. "Not Dad?"

CHAPTER IX

Chet, Rope Thrower

"Is DAD worse?" Frank gasped.

"I don't know," Chet replied. "All your mother said was to come to the hospital and hurry."

"Thanks," Frank said, starting the motor again. "We'll let you know if anything's wrong."

The coupé's speedometer hovered at the speed limit as the boys, fearful of what they might learn at the hospital, raced toward Bayport General Hospital.

When the boys arrived, they did not wait for the elevator, but took the stairs, three steps at a time. The brothers hastened down the corridor into their father's room.

Much to their surprise, they saw the detective propped up with pillows. He greeted them cheerfully.

"Hello, boys," he said. "Hope I didn't worry you by bringing you here so quickly."

"To be honest, Dad, you did," Frank panted. "It sure is good to see you so chipper, though."

Joe went to the far side of his father's bed and put his arm around the detective's broad shoulders. "Gosh, Dad, you look like yourself again. Doesn't he, Mother?"

Mrs. Hardy smiled in agreement. She was pouring water for one of the many bouquets her husband had received.

"I think your splendid detective work has helped your father immensely," she said. "He's very proud of you."

As Frank and Joe exchanged pleased glances, Mr. Hardy spoke up.

"The reason I called you boys," he said, "is this." The detective held up an air-mail letter. "It's from Cousin Ruth. She wants me to come immediately. Things at the ranch are going from bad to worse. You two had better not delay any longer. Forget the train reservations. I want you to fly out there at once."

"If those are orders, we'll go today," Frank said, smiling. "But Joe and I just got a hot lead on the crooked arrow mystery. We'd like to follow it up."

Fenton Hardy, knowing that his son was a born sleuth, understood the boy's reluctance to leave Bayport now. But the situation out West was pressing, too.

"I'll put Sam Radley to work on your new lead," Mr. Hardy said. "If the Arrow cigarette probe isn't complete by the time you get back, you can take it on again. Now tell me what you've learned."

Frank told about the Green Point tobacco dealer, then about Arrow Charlie and how he was expected back from Mexico soon. Mr. Hardy did not interrupt. At the end, he said:

"You know, I believe there is some connection between the case here and the one at Cousin Ruth's."

"How could there be?" Joe asked, amazed.

"Well," his father replied, "in the first place, that man who told you about Arrow Charlie may have misspoken. He may have meant that Arrow Charlie was coming here from *New* Mexico, instead of Mexico. But what's even more likely, someone may have been sent here from New Mexico to shoot me so I couldn't go out there. It may or it may not have any direct connection with Cousin Ruth's hard luck, but I'm sure now somebody doesn't want me in that vicinity."

"Well, we'll fool 'em," Frank said with determination. "Come on, Joe, we'll see about plane reservations."

The brothers hastily made their way to the Bayport airfield. Striding up to the ticket office, Frank and Joe approached the clerk at the window.

"We'd like three reservations to New Mexico as soon as we can get them," Frank said.

The clerk examined his schedule. "Sorry," he said. "Everything's booked up for a week."

"A week!" groaned Joe. "How about a plane to another point and a transfer?"

The clerk shook his head. "Not a chance," he said. "Schedule's full."

"All right," Frank said with a sigh. "Put us on the list for a cancellation."

As the boys walked out of the building, Joe's eyes suddenly lighted up. "I've got it. Why don't we charter a private plane, Frank?"

"Good idea," his brother agreed. "Let's inquire."

The boys saw a policeman at the side of the airfield and asked him about private planes. He directed them to a sleek two-engine job, where a man, astride the plane's nose, was tinkering with a motor.

"He might do it," the policeman said.

As the boys approached, the man climbed down a light metal ladder. "Something I can do for you?" he asked.

"We'd like to fly to New Mexico," Frank said. "Could you take us?"

"Sorry, I'm flying a businessman to South America, but I think maybe a fellow who came in today can help you out."

"Where is he?" Joe asked.

"Over in the lunchroom at the end of that runway," the man pointed. "He's short and dark, and has a mustache."

The boys thanked the flier and hurried to the lunchroom. They had no trouble spotting the pilot, a swarthy little man. He was eating a bowl of soup.

"Are you a private pilot?" Frank asked him.

The man brushed a crumb from his mustache. "Yeah. Why?" he asked.

"We'd like to fly to New Mexico. There'll be three of us. Could you take us?"

The flier looked the boys up and down. "Sure, I can take you," he said.

"Swell," Joe burst out. "When can we start?"

"Right now if you want to."

"Hold on a minute, Joe," cautioned his older brother. Then, turning to the man, Frank asked, "How much for the trip?"

The pilot avoided Frank's candid gaze, looking instead at his bowl of soup.

"Two thousand dollars," he said.

"Spin my prop!" Joe shouted. "Two thousand dollars?"

"That's right," the swarthy man replied. "Take it or leave it."

"We'll leave it, thank you," Frank said. "Come on, Joe. Let's look for another plane."

"You bet!" Joe exclaimed. "We don't want to buy this man's plane!"

Unfortunately, there were no other private pilots at the field. Frank and Joe got into their car and started home. After a mile on the highway, Frank said suddenly:

"Joe! I have an idea that pilot—"

"Yes?"

"I think he may be in cahoots with the crooked arrow gang."

"Why?" Joe asked, perplexed.

"No pilot would ask that much to fly us," Frank explained. "I'll bet he's deliberately trying to keep us from going to New Mexico as the archer did Dad."

"Let's go back and find out who he is," Joe suggested.

Frank made a U turn on the broad highway and headed back toward the airport. Whey they entered the lunchroom the pilot was gone. The man behind the counter said he had left in a hurry.

The Hardys dashed outside. The fellow was not in sight. They asked the flier who was still tinkering with the two-engine plane if he had seen the dark-skinned pilot.

"Yep," he replied. "There he is." He pointed to a speck in the sky. "Took off a few minutes ago."

"Who is he?" Frank asked.

"Dunno," was the answer.

The boys inquired at the office. Obligingly the clerk looked him up.

"He's Jack Howe, from New York City."

"Which proves exactly nothing," Frank declared.

Disappointed at their failure, either to advance a step in solving the mystery or getting reservations, the boys got back in their car. As Frank breezed along, Joe said:

"Let's drop by at Chet's and tell him to get ready. You know how poky he is."

"Right."

When they slowed down on the road fronting the Morton farm, a strange sight greeted their eyes. In a cow pasture among a herd of cows rode a cowboy on a chestnut mare.

"Yippee!" laughed Joe. "It's Chet!"

The boys stopped and got out.

"Hi, Chet! Where'd you get that rig?"

"Bought it, of course," puffed Chet.

He leaned over in the saddle and looked down at the Hardys. "I've been practicing for out West. Watch me rope a cow."

Chet swung a rope over his head, then flung it at a Holstein grazing complacently near by. The rope snaked through the air and landed smack over an old tree stump.

"Bull's-eye!" Joe shouted.

"Looks like you're stumped!" Frank wisecracked.

"That was only the first try," Chet retorted. "Watch this one."

He looped the rope again. It glided through the air, landing neatly over the cow's head.

"Told you!" he cried.

Chet should have been satisfied with this feat. But wishing to impress his audience, he yanked the rope, as he had seen cowboys do in the movies. With a toss of her head, the animal gave a loud, frightened bellow, and started to run.

Chet had been gazing at Frank and Joe, hoping to elicit a word of praise, and wasn't watching the cow. Suddenly, with a jerk, she pulled him from the horse.

With a thud, somewhat cushioned by his avoir- dupois, the boy landed in a clump of grass. The Hardys doubled over with laughter.

"Do it again," Joe egged him on. "I didn't see it."

He leaned over to help his friend off the ground. As he did so, the cow, tired of the whole silly busi- ness, butted Joe squarely!

CHAPTER X

Pursuit in the Clouds

"OOMPH!" Joe grunted as he sprawled in the pasture.

It was Chet's turn to laugh. The stout boy shook all over, like an old jalopy on a country road.

"A fine bunch of detectives we are!" Frank laughed. "If we don't keep our eyes open better than this, we'll never solve the mystery on Cousin Ruth's cattle ranch."

Joe, rising from the ground and brushing off his pants, addressed Chet. "Good thing that wasn't a bull," he said ruefully. Then he added, "Be ready to fly out West with us the minute we call you. Dad's much better. He wants us to start as soon as we can get reservations."

"Gee, that's swell," Chet beamed.

"Remember, no more than fifty pounds of luggage," Frank reminded him.

Chet wiped his brow with his red bandanna ker-chief. "Fifty pounds?" he exclaimed. "Why, my saddle and boots and duffel bag and . . . "

"And you," Joe teased, "all add up to about five hundred pounds!"

"No fooling," Frank said seriously, "you can't take all this equipment by plane."

"I'll send it by express," Chet decided.

"No go," his friend said. "Take too long out to those wilds."

"Then I'll have to buy all new stuff when I get there!" Chet wailed. "And I haven't any money left!"

"There's one sure way to get some," Joe sug-gested.

"How?" Chet asked eagerly.

"Earn it," Joe said, winking at his brother.

Chet's face dropped like a bulldogged calf. Then he remarked:

"I could have earned part of it, helping the farmer down the road build the foundation for his new barn. But there's not time enough."

"Hop to it," Joe said. "We may not go for a week."

Frank and Joe left their friend staring in be-wilderment. Definitely Chet did not like to work. What was he going to do?

With a sigh that could have been heard at the

next farm, he trudged down the road to carry stones for the farmer.

Chet came home that evening dusty and hot from the rugged work. The next morning he was up so early that he surprised even his mother. After putting away a breakfast of ham and eggs, griddle cakes, fruit, and a pint of milk, Chet hurried back to his job.

A big truck had dumped a huge pile of stones at the side of the road. It was Chet's chore to haul them in a wheelbarrow to the site of the new foundation. About midday, as he was working alone and figuring on how soon he could get off for a hearty lunch, a strange man approached him.

"Hi-ya," said the friendly Chet, eager for an excuse to rest from his weary task.

"Looks like you're workin' mighty hard," said the man.

He had broad shoulders, a large nose, and bushy black eyebrows.

"Yeah," Chet agreed. "It's tough work carrying these stones, 'specially when the sun's so hot."

"Well," the stranger replied, "a boy oughta help his father!"

"I'm not doing this for my father," Chet said, leaning against a fence post.

"Oh, no?" replied the man in surprise. "You're just workin' here?"

"There's a good reason," Chet said as a smile wreathed his round face. "I've got to make some money in a hurry."

"Hurry?" asked the man. "You got all summer, ain't you?"

"Nope," the boy replied, throwing out his chest pridefully. "I'm leaving any minute. Goin' out West."

"Is that a fact?" the stranger remarked. "What part of the West?"

The boy was so enthusiastic about his trip that he told the man all about Ruth Hardy having trouble at her ranch and how the Hardy boys were taking their father's place on the flight to investigate the peculiar goings-on at Crowhead.

A twisted smile, unnoticed by the stout boy, came to the man's lips as he urged Chet to go on with his story. When the boy had finished, the man tugged at the brim of his hat. Then, without even so much as a good-bye, he hurried down the road.

"Funny kind of a duck," Chet said to himself.

As he watched, the stranger walked under a low-hanging tree by the side of the road. An instant later the boy heard the roar of a motor and saw a car pull onto the road. It sped toward Bayport.

Pondering over the man's peculiar actions, Chet went back to his chore. Suddenly he let out a howl of dismay.

"My gosh," he thought. "That man! He was probably a spy!"

Chet loped home to telephone the Hardys.

Meanwhile, the Hardy home was as busy as rodeo day in a prairie town. The airline office had telephoned, offering three cancellations to El Paso the following evening. From there they could go north to Crowhead. Frank and Joe began packing their light equipment, relying on Cousin Ruth's cowboys to supply them with the bulkier things needed for ranch life.

"I've just got to take this saddle," Frank said, as he admired the Western saddle which he had kept in such good condition. By leaving out some less essential articles, he figured he might include the precious piece in his baggage.

"I'm nearly set!" Joe exclaimed presently. "It's sure going to feel good to be on a pony again!"

While they were busy, the telephone rang. Chet Morton was calling.

"Gosh, I've been trying for an hour to get you," he complained.

Frank, who had answered, realized the telephone had been busy. Many interested friends of the Hardys had been calling to inquire about the detective's condition.

"I got your message about the plane," he said.

"That's swell.   But say, I guess I pulled an awful boner."

He apologetically told about his talk with the stranger, and described him.

"Wow!" Frank exclaimed.   "He sounds like that man who came to Slow Mo's and tried to take the mystery car!"

"I shouldn't have opened my big mouth," Chet said in self-criticism.

After hanging up, Frank turned to Joe, told him the story, and added, "That guy is keeping close tabs on us.   I don't like it."

The boys had scarcely returned to their work when the doorbell rang.   Aunt Gertrude answered.

"Boys," she called, "come here!"

Hurrying to her side, Frank and Joe saw that she had a telegram in her hand.

"It's from Cousin Ruth," she said, passing it over to Frank.   The boy read it aloud with mingled feelings.   It said:

HAVE CHANGED MY PLANS.   DO NOT COME TO CROWHEAD.   RUTH

"Gosh!" Joe exclaimed.   "Just when we're all ready to go!"

"I wonder what happened?" Frank said, puzzled. "Things must have straightened out in a hurry."

"Nothing of the sort," declared Aunt Gertrude

emphatically. "Ruth is probably in the power of those bandits out there! It wouldn't surprise me if they made her send this wire!"

"You may be right," Frank said, secretly admiring his aunt's hunch. "Maybe Cousin Ruth was forced to tell us to cancel our trip."

"There's one way to find out," Frank put in. "Telephone Crowhead Ranch."

"It will cost a lot," his aunt said. "But that doesn't matter when the poor woman's life may be in danger! Frank, phone Cousin Ruth this minute!"

Her dark-haired nephew dialed long-distance. After a short delay he was connected with Crowhead Ranch, many hundreds of miles away.

"Hello. This is Frank, Cousin Ruth."

"How are you? When is your father coming out here?"

"Didn't you send him a wire saying not to come?"

"No. Certainly not. The quicker he gets here the better."

"He's not coming; we are," Frank told his cousin. "Dad is ill. We'll tell you all about it when we see you," Frank added quickly to forestall any questions. "We'll be there the day after tomorrow. Good-bye."

When he told his brother what Cousin Ruth had said, Joe exciaimed, "An enemy of Cousin Ruth must have forged the telegram. I can't wait to get there now."

Late the next afternoon Frank and Joe, accompanied by their mother and their aunt, went to the hospital to say good-bye to their father. Mr. Hardy was in good spirits. The doctor had said he could go home the following day.

"Keep your eyes and ears open, boys," he advised, "and look for the unusual. I'm sure you'll be able to clear up what's worrying Cousin Ruth."

"We'll do our best, Dad," Frank replied.

"Don't take any unnecessary risks," the detective cautioned as his sons left. "And keep me posted on what's happening."

When the brothers reached the airport, Chet was there, grinning gleefully under a ten-gallon hat. After fond farewells to their families, the three boys boarded the plane. In a few moments the engines roared and the big craft soared into the sky. Bayport became a speck in the distance, finally disappearing on the horizon.

The plane made several stops across the country, arriving very early the next morning at El Paso, Texas. The boys got off and looked around for a small charter craft to fly them to Crowhead. When Frank entered the administration building for information, a man approached him.

"You looking for a charter plane?" he asked.

"Yes," the boy replied. "How did you know?"

"Just saw you fellows get off the transport," he replied. "Judging from the way you looked around, I figured you were hankering for a charter hop."

"That's right," said Frank. "Where can I get a plane?"

The man looked pleased. "A friend of mine has a nifty ship," he said. "He'll take you wherever you want to go. And very reasonable, too."

Something about the man's overeagerness aroused Frank's suspicions.

"I have something to attend to first," the boy said. "I'll talk to you later if we want to engage your friend."

When Frank told Chet and his brother about the man's offer, they agreed that they had best be wary of the fellow.

"We'd better be careful of every move," Frank cautioned. "Let's look around to see what else is for hire."

"Not me," Chet put in. "That breakfast on the plane wasn't enough. I'm going to drop in the restaurant here for a bite."

The boy disappeared into the airport cafeteria while Frank and Joe strolled off to find a charter plane. Chet had just finished two orders of pancakes when he happened to glance out the window alongside him.

What he saw almost made him choke. There was the man he had spoken to at the roadside in Bayport!

"I've got to tell the Hardys!" Chet thought.

At that moment the man turned, his eyes meeting those of Chet for a split second. He did not look back.

"I don't think he recognized me," Chet told himself.

The stranger moved on, disappearing around a corner. Chet paid his check and hurried from the restaurant. It took him ten minutes to find Frank and Joe. They were talking to a young pilot standing beside a small cabin plane. Quickly he motioned Frank aside and told him about the stranger.

"That doesn't sound good." Frank frowned. "There's no doubt we've been followed." Then he turned to the pilot. "Mr. Winger, I'd like you to meet our friend Chet Morton. He's making the flight to Crowhead with us."

Chet shook hands with the airman as Joe said, "Mr. Winger is a former Army pilot. He's taking us to Cousin Ruth's place."

"Swell," Chet beamed.

The pilot helped his passengers pack their luggage in the plane. Then, taxiing to the end of the runway, he turned, headed into the wind and took off smoothly.

"These small planes are great," Joe said enthusiastically.

"Just as safe as the big airliners," Frank said confidently. Chet wished he could agree. He was holding on tightly to the sides of his seat, gazing at the ground below.

"Take your eyes off the scenery," Frank advised, "and look at the clouds!"

Chet turned. Looking backward, he suddenly motioned to the boys excitedly.

"Hey!" he yelled. "I think a plane's following us."

The pilot turned, and agreed. He slowed his roaring motor.

"We'll let him catch up so we can take a look-see. Maybe it's a friend of mine having some fun."

"Or somebody looking for trouble," Joe said grimly.

The plane tailing the Hardys' craft also relaxed its pace, keeping in back and slightly above them.

Frank told Winger just enough of the mystery they were trying to solve to interest him in helping the boys.

"I'm sure that plane is following us for no good reason," he said.

When the pilot heard this, he asked, "Want to change about?"

"What do you mean?" Frank asked.

"I'll get in back of that guy and follow him," the pilot said. Then he added, "How's your stomach?"

Frank smiled and Joe answered, "Okay with us. How about you, Chet?"

The boy groaned. The pancakes felt like lead under his belt, but he nodded to go ahead.

"Get set!" the pilot shouted.

Suddenly the plane shot upward with such velocity that the boys felt as if they were being pressed into their seats by an invisible hand.

In a breath-taking swoop, the craft was upside down in a tight inside loop. Then it swooped down directly in back of the other plane!

CHAPTER XI

The Face at the Window

TAKEN by surprise, the pilot in the plane ahead of the Hardy boys tried to shake off Winger's ship. It banked first to the right, then to the left. But the former Army man stuck to his quarry.

"Atta boy!" Joe cried gleefully, admiring the deft maneuvering of the pilot.

Chet did not say a word. His eyes stared straight ahead as if they were glued to a specter.

Finally the kibitzing plane, after zooming in vain to get away from the boys' aircraft, headed back toward El Paso. Winger followed. The pursued ship headed directly for the airport and descended.

Winger remained aloft for a few minutes until the tower gave him permission to land. Just as he touched the wheels of his plane to the runway, the boys saw the other plane make a daring take-off.

"Follow him!" Joe cried.

"I can't chase him now," the pilot replied. "Against regulations to go up without checking in."

"Bet that fellow didn't," Joe said.

When Frank, Joe, and the pilot entered the administration building, they found a group of angry officials discussing the mysterious plane which had broken the rules of the field so boldly. It had come in without a signal and taken off without reporting!

Unfortunately no one had noticed its number. The plane had swooped in and out so fast that it had eluded detection.

Frank related the story of their experience. They could offer little to identify it. Neither Winger nor the boys had noticed the number of the mysterious aircraft. Maybe it had none! The officials promised to do all they could to trace the lawbreaking pilot and his plane.

"Well, let's start all over again," Winger proposed as the three walked back to their own craft.

"I hope Chet hasn't run off." Joe grinned. "I don't think he and his pancakes liked your air circus."

But Chet was in the seat where they had left him.

"How do you feel?" Winger asked him.

Chet bobbed his head up and down, saying nothing.

A few minutes later they were in the air. Here and there dense woodlands crept into view, dotting the hills and cattle country. Once in a while a picturesque ranch house came into view below.

"According to your directions, we should be headed straight for Crowhead," Winger said an hour later. "Ever been here before by air?" he asked.

"No."

"Well, if you recognize anything about the ranch, let me know."

Frank and Joe became more alert to the terrain unfolding beneath them. Presently the plane droned over a dense woodland of ponderosa pines.

Frank, glancing from the right side of the craft, abruptly reached out and grabbed Joe's arm. At the same time he shouted:

"Hey, look at that!"

"What is it?" Winger queried, while Joe jumped up and looked out Frank's window.

"There among the trees," Frank pointed.

Joe and the pilot scanned the woods. Chet was too busy thinking about his pancakes to pay much attention.

"I see it!" Joe exclaimed. "It's a giant arrow cut out of the woods," he cried excitedly.

"And it's crooked!" Frank observed.

Winger was puzzled. "How the deuce could that happen?" he asked.

He banked to go back and look at the strange

sight again. By this time Chet's curiosity was aroused, and he, too, looked and exclaimed in amazement.

"It looks," said Frank, "as if the timber had been cut purposely in the form of an S-shaped arrow."

"So it does," the pilot commented. "Never saw it before, but then I seldom fly over this country."

"Let's circle around to see if we can spot any more arrows," Joe suggested.

"Okay with me," the pilot agreed, "if you've got the time. I have plenty."

Winger flew in ever-widening circles. The dense woodland was unbroken by any other arrows etched in the deep greenery.

Finally, the pilot came back again to the crooked arrow. Frank nudged Joe, who bent his head closer to his brother.

"Do you see where the arrow points?" he whispered excitedly.

"Right toward Crowhead Ranch!" Joe answered.

"I'm afraid," Frank said, "that Crowhead is a marked ranch!"

"But why?" Joe puzzled. "What possible connection could there be between a knockout cigarette and a cattle ranch?"

"When we know that, Joe, I'll feel a lot easier about the safety of the Hardy family," his brother replied.

"I wish we could go down and see if anybody lives here," Joe said. "It might be a hide-out for the crooked arrow gang!"

"No chance of landing among these trees," Frank declared.

As the pilot headed away from the woodland arrow, Joe noticed a cleared spot beyond the arrow's head. It was barely large enough for a plane to land, and a take-off would be almost impossible.

Nevertheless Joe was about to point out the spot to Winger with the idea of a possible landing, when suddenly the airplane's motor began to sputter. The flier looked back at the boys, his forehead wrinkled with anxiety.

"I may have to take her down!" he called grimly.

Winger worked frantically, but the engine failed to respond. With a sickly wheeze, it conked out.

The sudden silence brought Chet out of his squeamish disinterest in the trip.

"Gee!—Oh, gosh!"

The wind whined against the plane's surfaces as the craft, under Winger's steady hand, made for the clearing that Frank had seen. Chet closed his eyes, but the Hardys, fascinated by the flier's skill, watched every move.

The plane banked, nearly crashing into the tree-tops. At last it settled down in the clearing without overturning.

"Whew!" Chet cried out. "That was too close for comfort!"

"Sure was," said Winger. "And I hope we can get out of here."

They all jumped from the plane. Frank offered to help examine the engine for the trouble spot. He was an expert mechanic as a result of having taken so many jalopies apart and put them together again.

"Joe, how about you and Chet taking a look around to see if anyone lives in these woods?" he suggested.

"Okay," his brother agreed.

Chet stared at the unknown and, he figured, perhaps hostile surroundings. He was not of a mind to move one foot.

"A walk will do you good," Joe urged.

Chet remained where he was. "I knew it," he said. "I come out West for a good time, and the first thing I know I'm in a gangsters' hide-out."

"That shouldn't bother you. How about that judo you learned?" Joe needled him. "You could throw a couple of gunmen right over your shoulder."

"G-gunmen?" Chet stuttered. "That settles it. I'll help on the motor. You and Frank go."

The boy could not be persuaded to leave, so the Hardys went off together. They advanced among the trees cautiously, but there were no signs of human habitation.

Someone had been at the spot within a few weeks, however, because the land in the crooked arrow area had been stripped of all new growth, evidently to keep the arrow sign in plain sight from the air.

"This spot is just a marker for members of the crooked arrow gang flying over it," Frank concluded.

The boys hunted for any clues to the crooks' identity but found nothing. Finally they returned to the plane. Winger had located the trouble. It was in the fuel line.

"Nobody around," Joe reported, "but from the cuts on the stumps, it's a sure bet those trees were felled on purpose. It was no natural phenomenon."

"Whoever did it surely went to a lot of trouble," commented Winger, as he tightened a coupling in the fuel pipe. A few minutes later he said, "Well, we're ready to take off. The really tough job's ahead; to get out of here." He eyed the length of the clearing. "If we're lucky, we can make it," he said. "But I wish we could throw off some excess weight."

Joe eyed Chet slyly.

"No, not me!" the boy protested, then grinned foolishly for having fallen for Joe's quip.

They climbed into the plane, and Winger took his place at the controls. The pilot taxied to the end of the clearing and turned, taking advantage of every inch of ground. He applied the brakes until the motor roared, then zipped down the natural runway.

The boys held their breaths as the plane sped toward the trees at the far end of the open space. Suddenly, with a bound like a high jumper, the craft nosed up sharply. Boughs clutched at the underside of the fuselage, but the ship soared into the sky unscathed. Winger was perspiring as he leveled off.

"That sure was swell," Frank praised him, and the others added words of commendation. It was late afternoon when the plane landed at Crowhead, without further adventure. Frank had identified the ranch from the layout of the buildings, and Winger had set the wheels down on a big field alongside the house.

Chet eyed his surroundings with suspicious alarm. He half expected a band of Indians with poisoned arrows to rush out and start shooting.

Instead, everything seemed to be peaceful. Half a dozen friendly cowhands ambled toward the plane. Upon learning Frank and Joe were nephews of Mrs. Ruth Hardy, they took out the luggage and two of the men preceded the boys to the house with it.

Frank paid Winger, and they said good-bye, as he wanted to get back to El Paso before dark.

Two other cowhands escorted the three boys to the ranch house. Cousin Ruth met them at the door.

"It's a shame about your dad," she exclaimed, "but I'm glad to see you boys, anyway."

The boys introduced Chet to their relative, who had changed considerably since they had last seen her. Cousin Ruth's hair, once blond, now was streaked with gray, and her face was careworn from the ordeal of her husband's death and the responsibilities of the ranch. She said nothing about her worries, however.

After the visitors had been shown to two well-furnished bedrooms, they were invited to a sumptuous lunch. Chet was in his glory.

"Golly," he beamed, seeing the platter of steaks, "Bayport was never like this!"

When the meal was over, the boys walked around to get acquainted with the place. It was not until dusk had fallen and work had ceased for the night that Ruth Hardy met them again and brought up the subject which the boys were so eager to hear.

They had gathered in her attractive living room. The widow closed the door, glanced furtively out the window, then launched into the story of the difficulties at Crowhead. The boys leaned forward attentively.

"One by one my best cowboys have been disappearing," Cousin Ruth said. "They leave very mysteriously, taking their saddles and all their clothing with them."

"And don't tell you they're going?" Frank asked.

"They tell no one. As a result, Hank, my foreman, hasn't been able to get all the ranch work done."

"Can't you hire new hands?" Joe spoke up.

"They won't work here," their cousin replied. "We've advertised. The story has got around that Crowhead is—well—jinxed. Nobody has heard from the men who disappear."

"What do the police say?" Joe asked.

"The sheriff," said the widow, "has done all he can to solve the mystery, but the men keep vanishing into thin air."

As Cousin Ruth talked, night dropped into the valley. She switched on the living-room light, at the same time saying: "You boys must be tired. Perhaps you had better go to bed. We get up very early here."

"And I'd like to do some watching early in the morning," Frank said. "Come on, fellows."

As he rose from his chair, he glanced out the window. A pair of unfriendly eyes was peering into the room! Then a forehead ducked down and disappeared.

CHAPTER XII

A Suspicious Foreman

"SOMEBODY is spying on us already!" Frank thought.

He sidled over to the window, but whoever had been peering through it had disappeared. Excusing himself from his hostess, Frank ran to the kitchen, then out the back door. He hoped, by doubling back, to catch the intruder unawares.

The boy made his way quietly around the building. Nobody was near the window.

As Frank listened for a sound to indicate the eavesdropper's whereabouts, he heard hoofbeats. They seemed to come from the direction of the corral, then rumble off in the distance like the muffled beat of a drum.

"He got away in a hurry," Frank thought in disgust.

When he returned inside, Cousin Ruth asked him what had happened. Not wishing to worry her, the boy merely said he had heard a noise and won-dered about it.

Frank kept his discovery secret until he and Joe were alone in their room. Chet already had tum-bled into bed, and his gentle snoring indicated he was sound asleep.

"I think we'd better not alarm Cousin Ruth," Frank said when he had completed his story, and Joe agreed. "But there's something I'd like to ask her before we turn in," he added, as an idea came to him.

Seeing a light still on in the living room, he went to find his cousin. She was reading.

"Oh," she said in surprise, "would you boys like a snack before retiring? I forgot to ask you."

"No, thank you," Frank replied. "Joe and I were talking about the mystery. We wondered how many horses are in the corral. Seems like an awful lot of them."

"We have twenty-five now," Mrs. Hardy said, a note of sadness in her voice. "We used to have many more, but conditions here forced me to sell them."

Frank said good night again and went to his room, and suggested a plan to Joe.

Instead of undressing, the Hardys turned out their light and waited. In a few minutes their cousin went to her bedroom. Half an hour later

Crowhead Ranch was cloaked in dense stillness, broken only by the chirping of crickets and the occasional mournful howl of a coyote.

"Let's go now," Frank whispered.

The boys tiptoed to the kitchen and opened the back door. Making their way to the corral, they could hear the slight noise of the horses, who sensed the presence of strangers.

"Hope they don't rouse anybody," Frank whispered.

Just then the moon, whose ghostly light had been concealed behind a mass of somber clouds, broke into the open sky. In the dim glow cast over the corral, Frank and Joe could see the horses.

"We'll both count 'em," Frank said.

After a moment of silence, Joe whispered, "Twenty-four!"

"That's what I get!" Frank replied.

"There's one missing," Joe said excitedly.

"That might mean," Frank reasoned, "that the person who looked in the window and rode off works for Crowhead."

"Listen!" Joe warned suddenly.

The boys held their breaths, intent on catching the sound that Joe had picked up.

"I hear it!" Frank said hoarsely. "It's a rider. Maybe the same one coming back!"

The brothers raced into the shadow of a shed which stood near the corral, and waited. The hoofbeats grew closer. A few minutes later a cowboy reined in his mount at the corral gate and flung himself off the saddle. Lifting the bar, he slapped his horse on the rump and the animal bounded inside.

All the while, Frank and Joe craned their necks to get a glimpse of the stranger. But a deep shadow, thrown by his broad-brimmed hat, concealed the face of the rider.

The boys noted that he was tall and rangy, but so were many other cowboys. If only they could get a good look at him!

The man hastened toward the bunkhouse. As he neared the hiding place of the Hardys, Frank and Joe flattened themselves against the side of the building. The beating of their hearts sounded like trip hammers in their ears.

When the cowboy passed them, he suddenly whipped off his hat, wiping his brow with the back of his wrist. The moon shone full on his face. It revealed a thin nose and jutting jaw, giving his face the sour demeanor of a man who is dissatisfied with the whole world.

He hurried on, and soon the boys heard the bunkhouse door shut lightly after him. When all was quiet again, the brothers made their way silently to the house.

"We'll spot him in the morning," Frank whispered. "Something's up!"

They opened the back door, which they had left ajar. Then, taking off their shoes, they crept back to their room.

In the morning the brothers were awakened by the bright sun. It burst into their window with a brilliance unlike that in Bayport.

"Swell country, this," Joe commented.

"Sure is. We've got to see to it Cousin Ruth doesn't lose this ranch," Frank declared.

The Hardys roused Chet, who rolled sleepily from bed.

"Hi, it's time to get up," Joe said, as he prodded his friend.

"Lemme sleep," Chet protested.

"You're going to miss breakfast," Frank teased. "They don't serve it in bed, you know."

Hearing the word breakfast, the stocky boy quickly shook off his drowsiness and dressed. Cousin Ruth greeted them in the living room.

"While breakfast is being cooked," she said, "suppose we go outside and I'll introduce you to the men."

They stepped onto a rambling porch, which shaded one side of the building, then walked toward the bunkhouse. A group of cowboys, whom the Easterners had not seen the day before, were making ready for their day's work.

"I'd like you to meet my two cousins Frank and Joe and their friend, Chet," the widow said pleasantly, approaching the cowboys. "They're from Bayport and are spending a little vacation with us."

"Howdy," said the men, shaking hands with the trio.

Ruth Hardy introduced them one by one. Presently she stopped beside a little fellow with shiny, black braids falling over each shoulder. His leathery face was as weather-beaten as a mountain rock, but the crinkly expression around his eyes indicated a keen sense of humor.

"I know you'll like Crowhead's Pye," their cousin said, turning to the boys.

"Pie?" Chet said enthusiastically. "Are we going to have pie for breakfast?"

A few of the cowboys laughed. The others registered a look of disgust.

"No." The woman smiled. "This is Pye. P-Y-E. His real name is Pymatuno, and he's the best Indian in all of New Mexico!"

A broad smile forced Pye's eyes into little slits as he shook hands with the boys. Then Cousin Ruth looked around, as if she had missed somebody.

"Where's Hank?" she asked. Turning to her

visitors, Mrs. Hardy said, "He's my foreman."

As she spoke, the bunkhouse door slammed and a tall man emerged. He had a thin nose and jutting jaw.

The cowboy was the mysterious rider of the night before! As he approached the group, Ruth Hardy introduced him.

"Howdy," he said, extending a long, bony hand and showing no enthusiasm at the meeting.

"Up purty early for city kids, ain't yo'?" he commented, looking at the trio with a poker face.

The boys resented the cutting remark, especially Joe, who wasn't endowed with the same even temper as his older brother.

"It seems to me," he came back pointedly, "that certain cowboys as well as city folks stay out late at night!"

Hank tensed. The muscles in his lean cheeks bulged in and out.

"Sometimes," he snapped, "a cowboy has to run coyotes off the place."

Just then the mellow strum of a guitar eased the situation. A pint-sized cowboy, wearing a bright red-and-yellow shirt, walked from the bunkhouse.

"That's Terry," Ruth Hardy said.

"He's mighty fleet-fingered with the gee-tar," one of the men spoke up.

"I don't know what I'd do without Terry."

Cousin Ruth smiled. "He's a joy, but an awful tease."

The singing cowboy grinned, showing a straight set of white teeth. He strummed a few chords, then said, looking directly at the visitors from Bay-port:

"Howdy, howdy, all o' you," then broke into song.

> *Ef yo' wanna be a cowman,*
> *Yippee, yippee-yay,*
> *Yo' gotta ride to beat the band*
> *Every single day.*
> *But take a soft guy from the city*
> *Ah, how his hoss will play,*
> *It shore will be a pity*
> *When his rider hits the sand!*

Terry gaily twanged out an extra chord as the cowboys roared with laughter.

"Oh, we can ride some," Frank volunteered with a laugh.

"If yo' can't, then we'll larn yo'," Terry said.

At that moment the ranch house bell rang. Ruth Hardy and the "city soft guys," their faces red, went off to breakfast. When they finished, Frank took his cousin aside in one corner of the room, and said:

"I don't mind being razzed because I'm from

the city, but it seemed to me that your foreman Hank was not kidding us. Is he always like that?"

"Oh, Hank's all right," their cousin assured the boy. "He's a little dictatorial, but I think Hank means well enough."

"Seems mighty queer to me," Frank said with a worried frown. "Maybe your men are leaving on account of him."

"I hardly think so. Hank just doesn't like what he calls 'city dudes.' I'm sure you can grow to be friends, though."

"I hope so," Frank said. But the boy was afraid that his cousin's foreman might be mixed up in some way with the strange disappearance of the Crowhead cowboys.

Frank strolled onto the porch and told Joe of their cousin's confidence in Hank. Joe shrugged.

"Just the same," he suggested, "I think we'd better start looking for clues right now, and we'll not leave Hank out."

"Say, where did Chet vanish?" Frank asked aloud.

Ruth Hardy, coming outside, laughingly called from the doorway, "He ate a little too much breakfast to go riding just now, he said."

"We'll leave him here," Joe decided, "while Frank and I take a look around Crowhead."

"Hank will give you horses," Mrs. Hardy said.

The brothers walked to the corral, eager to ride over the meandering acres of Crowhead in search of clues to their cousin's mystery. When they asked for horses, Hank lifted the corral bar and went inside. He returned with two lively mounts.

"Saddle 'em yoreselves," he said gruffly.

The horses pranced and pawed, but finally the boys got the saddles strapped in place. Hank looked amazed, and as the brothers swung into their seats he watched intently.

Suddenly a figure raced toward them—it was Pye, the Indian.

"No ride!" he shouted excitedly. "Bad horse."

Hank glared at the Indian.

"Yo' stay out o' this!" he ordered.

As he spoke, Joe's horse reared. The next instant the animal did a sunfish, tossing Joe off his back into the dust!

CHAPTER XIII

The Whizzing Arrow

HANK guffawed at Joe's bad spill but made no attempt to subdue the rearing horse.

It was Pye who rushed in and grabbed the animal's bridle, yanking him and his crashing hoofs away from the boy.

With a cry Frank had dismounted and rushed to his brother. But Joe picked himself up and brushed the dirt from his jeans.

Hank's laughter suddenly turned into an angry frown as he saw Terry, the singing cowboy, approaching with two other horses.

"Who told yo' to bring 'em?" he shouted.

The little cowboy grinned, at the same time letting forth in a high tenor voice:

> *Yo' can't ride a bronc*
> *The very first day*
> *Yippity-yay. Yippitay-yay!*

"Shut up!" Hank bellowed. "Yo're not gettin' paid for singin'."

"I'm only tryin' to make the boys feel at home," Terry said.

"Leave that to me," the foreman snarled.

He turned to Pye, who had led the mean horses back into the corral.

"Look here, Indian," he snapped. "Get these tenderfeet to work ridin' fence."

"Me savvy," Pye replied. "Take other men along, too?"

"I can't spare any good men," Hank sneered at the Indian. "Now get goin'!"

The foreman strode off, leaving the boys with Pye. He offered to saddle the new mounts, but Frank and Joe cinched their own.

Pye mounted a little pinto and the three started for the fences.

"Boys good riders." Pye grinned in surprise, seeing the ease with which the Hardys handled their mounts.

"We've done some riding back East," Frank replied.

"Nice paint you got there, Pye," Joe said admiringly.

Pye and his horse moved in perfect rhythm. It looked as if he and the little animal had been born riding together.

"Him fine horse," the Indian said proudly. "Him know two language—white man and Navaho."

With that he spoke an Indian word. The pinto stopped and dropped to his forelegs. Then Pye spoke in English. The pony arose and started off again.

Pye looked at the boys gleefully. "See?" he said. "Pony ver-y smart. Never go to school, either."

The boys laughed. "What's his name?" Frank asked as they cantered along.

"Cherry," the Indian replied. "Cowboy make fun with Pymatuno. Call Pye and horse Cherry Pye." The friendly Navaho grinned until his eyes almost disappeared.

The country over which the three rode was rough and scrubby. Here and there a few cattle grazed on the green patches which dotted the terrain.

Pye's admiration of the boys' horsemanship was unbounded. Finding that they showed no signs of fatigue, he urged them toward the northern fence line of the ranch.

"Nice up there," he said. "Long time ago Indian live there."

As they neared the boundary, Frank thought he heard the distant hum of a motor. He called his brother's attention to it.

"Sounds like a plane," Joe remarked, scanning the sky.

They knew that occasionally a transport passed over the area, flying at a very high altitude. But this one was low.

"There's plane," Pye declared, pointing over a wooded section a few miles ahead of them.

A small craft suddenly appeared and skimmed over the treetops.

"Joe!" Frank cried. "Isn't that the same one . . . ?"

"Golly," Joe cut in, "it sure looks like it!"

The boys could not make out the details of the airplane, but from a distance it could well be the same one which had followed them from El Paso the day before. Was the pilot searching for the Hardys? This thought was dispelled by a remark from the Indian.

"Me see plane many time," Pye said slowly. "All time he fly low by trees."

Frank and Joe exchanged glances. Was it in some way connected with the mysterious disappearance of the Crowhead cowboys? Perhaps it was landing near by, taking the ranch hands off to some other part of the country. Help was scarce in other range areas of the great West.

Suddenly Joe reined in sharply. "Look, Frank,"

he cried excitedly. "The plane's coming down."

The three watched as the craft banked and disappeared behind the trees.

"Do you suppose it's in trouble?" Joe asked his brother.

"Could be," Frank replied. "But it looked to me as if the pilot meant to land."

"In any case, I think we ought to find out," Joe declared.

But hardly were the words out of his mouth, when the plane zoomed sharply into the air.

"It didn't land after all," Joe commented. "What'd you make out of that?"

"Maybe him just have fun," the Indian said with a grin.

"Why would a pilot fool around out here?" Frank queried. "He'd be in serious trouble if he crashed. This country is too wooded to try any hopping."

As the stranger flew away, Frank noticed something that confirmed his belief the plane was not out on a playful junket. The sun's rays were reflected in the lenses of what was probably binoculars!

Joe saw it at the same time. "He's looking for something, Frank."

"And that something may be us," his brother replied with a frown.

"No worry," the Indian said. "He come back."

By this time he and the boys were nearing the woods. Pye hesitated, asking if the brothers wanted to ride into it. Wishing to learn where the airman had come down, they nodded.

As they entered the dark stillness, Frank felt a peculiar sensation. The trees, although not the tallest he had seen, appeared to stretch their limbs grotesquely toward the riders. Their gnarled branches, disfigured by wind and storm, seemed to beckon the boys into a trap which nature itself had devised.

"This sure is a spooky place," Joe remarked, feeling the same awesomeness.

"Very bad," Pye said. "Cowboys sometimes get lost in here." Then he grinned. "Pye no get lost."

Buoyed by the Indian's confidence, the boys entered the woods, ducking low-hanging branches along a faintly marked trail. Suddenly the pinto whinnied and stopped. Pye jumped off and put his ear to the ground.

"Someone come!" he warned.

The boys dismounted, leading their animals off the trail. As they did, a cowboy, panting as if he had run for miles, came stumbling along the path like a tumbleweed in a high wind. A sudden look of recognition came over the Indian's face.

"Pete!" he shouted.

The runner was one of the men from Crowhead. The cowboy stopped, a wild look in his eyes. "Where are you going?" Frank asked.

"Ch-chasin' my pony," Pete replied. "He—uh—run away."

"We no see him," Pye said. "No come this way."

"Here," Frank offered, "climb up and ride back of me. We'll take you home. It's a long way."

"No," the man replied. His shifting eyes looked right and left into the woods. "I'll keep on lookin' for him."

With that he started off again along the trail and disappeared in the woods.

"I'm going to follow him," Frank said after a few minutes. "This looks mighty suspicious."

"Pye and I'll stay here awhile and see if anyone else comes along," Joe said. "Pete may have been running away to meet somebody."

Frank wheeled his horse, heading after the disappearing Pete. When he was out of sight of Joe and Pye, Frank glanced at the ground, hoping to pick up some information as to Pete's strange behavior. What he saw suddenly sent a quiver of excitement racing down his spine.

At the base of a pine tree lay a large, smooth rock. On its face was carved a crooked arrow!

Frank bent low in his saddle to get a better look

at it. As he did so, an object whizzed above him.
It sounded like the buzz of a giant bee.

An instant later something sang closer to the boy's
head. It was followed by a zinging thud. An
arrow embedded itself in a tree trunk directly in
front of him!

Another zing! Frank fell to the ground!

CHAPTER XIV

Chet Snares a Clue

FRANK struck the ground with a thud and lay still. He had made it just in time to escape being wounded by an arrow, which barely missed his shoulder. Now he flattened out to make himself as inconspicuous a target as possible for his unseen assailant.

Ten minutes went by. No more arrows shot past him. Cautiously Frank raised his head to look through the brush. Not twenty feet away lay a short arrow. Near its nock were three white feathers.

"The same kind of arrow that hit Dad!" Frank told himself in amazement.

The boy pulled himself along the ground and grasped the shaft. No doubt of it. This arrow was a duplicate of the other. Probably it had come from the same quiver! But why had the archer traveled from Bayport to the wilds of New Mexico?

Cautiously Frank arose and looked around. He saw nobody. Then he wrapped the arrow in his kerchief and tied it to the saddle.

Frank spotted another arrow embedded in a tree a few yards away. From its position, he figured approximately the point from which the missile had been shot.

Keeping his eyes open for any human movement among the trees, Frank skirted the direct line of attack and approached the place from the rear. But when the boy reached the small clearing, where the assailant apparently had stood, he found no one.

Returning to his horse, Frank patted the animal's neck, all the while meditating the strange turn of events. The shooting in Bayport and the peculiar cigarettes the crooks were using definitely tied in with some strange plot against Ruth Hardy.

The giant crooked arrow sign cut in the timber, the crooked arrow chipped into the rock, and now the white-feathered shafts' seemed to fit into the same frightening pattern. But the mystery remained as deep and foreboding as the woods in which Frank stood.

He racked his brain trying to find the answer. Finally the boy decided to telephone his father to see if he had any connecting links to offer.

Frank's thoughts were interrupted by the sounds

of approaching footsteps. Perhaps Pete was returning. Or could it be the mysterious archer?

The boy quickly led his horse into a gully, then dived into a tangle of underbrush to await developments.

To his relief, he saw Joe and Pye suddenly appear among the trees. From Joe's interested look, Pye was apparently telling him some bit of Western lore. Frank startled them when he sidled into their path.

"Him quiet like redskin," Pye said with a grin.

"You'd be silent, too," Frank replied, "if somebody had stalked through the woods, taking pot shots at you with a bow and arrow!"

The Indian looked puzzled as Frank told his story.

"Nobody at Crowhead use arrow," Pye declared.

"Are you the only Indian there?" Joe asked.

Pye nodded. "No more Indian work for Mis' Hardy."

"Is there an Indian reservation near here?" Frank queried.

For a moment Pye was thoughtful. "Reservation hundred mile away," he replied.

"Then Indians wouldn't be wandering around here," Joe reasoned.

"Follow me," Frank said to the others.

He led the way to the stone into which the crooked arrow symbol had been cut, and pointed

to it. The boy watched Pye's expression intently.
It reflected the same amazement that Joe's did.

"Ever see this before or one like it?" Frank asked
him, although he was sure the answer would be no.

"Pye never see bad arrow. Indian no make bad
arrow," he said proudly, and added, grinning, "only
white man."

White man!

The remark gave the Hardys food for thought.
After the report on the wrist-watch strap, it had
been assumed that the dangerous archer was an
Indian. But if redskins had such contempt for
crooked arrows, then it was possible only white men
were involved in the baffling mystery, and were
trying to mislead Detective Fenton Hardy and his
sons into thinking Indians were the crooks. Probably the watch strap had belonged to an Indian at
one time.

"Go back to ranch house now," said Pye. "Long
ride."

The three headed back. There was little conversation on the way. After several hot, tedious hours
on horseback, they reached the inviting coolness of
Crowhead's buildings.

Frank went straight to the bunkhouse to find
Hank. The foreman eyed the boy suspiciously.

"What's the matter now?" he asked. "Yo' got
good horses, didn't yo'?"

"I'm looking for Pete," Frank said, ignoring the question. "Did he get back? We saw him in the woods some time ago. Said he had lost his horse and was looking for it."

"Pete's been gone since early morning," Hank scowled. "Now don't bother me again."

The evening wore on. Still Pete had not returned. Frank and Joe learned that the cowboy's horse had trotted back, but without a saddle.

Ruth Hardy was very upset. Pete was one of her most intelligent hands. According to the other men, he had seemed happy and satisfied at Crowhead.

"I can't understand it," Ruth said to Frank. "You see what happens. One day a man is here, the next he's gone with no explanation."

Frank said he wanted to report to his father, and put in the call to home. Mr. Hardy answered. His voice sounded strong and clear as he spoke to both his sons. He said that he was feeling better and asked what had been going on at the ranch.

Frank outlined the mysterious happenings. When he told of the stone in the woods with the crooked arrow on it, the boy could sense that his father was surprised.

"Did that arrow and the one you saw from the air point in the same direction?" he asked.

"Why, yes, they did, Dad," Frank replied.

"Then keep looking for more clues in that

woods," the detective advised. "But proceed carefully, and don't go far without someone trustworthy from Crowhead."

"It'll probably be Pye. He's a swell fellow."

After the boys had finished their story, Mr. Hardy brought them up to date on the mystery from the Bayport angle. The car in Slow Mo's garage was still unclaimed. Tobacco Shop Al remained silent. No more telltale wrist watches had been located, but the telephone wire fairly crackled with the electrifying news—it had been found that the Arrow cigarettes contained a mysterious gas!

"Sam Radley and government agents," Mr. Hardy said, "have arrested several peddlers of Arrow cigarettes in the Bayport area and in other widely scattered sections of the country. But they haven't nabbed the ringleader, whoever he is.

"Maybe he's Arrow Charlie," Frank suggested.

"We have a trap set for him if he shows up here," the detective said. "But he may show up nearer you. Watch your step!"

The boys promised they would, and the conversation ended. Frank and Joe spent the evening near the corral and the bunkhouse but learned nothing. No riders came in or went out up to twelve o'clock, and Pete did not return. Finally the brothers went to bed.

Chet Morton was up early with the Hardys the

next morning.   Having felt ill all the day before from overeating, he attacked his breakfast with some restraint.

"What's the matter, Chet?" Joe needled him, as the boys rose from the table.   "Lost your Eastern appetite?"

"I'm taking it easy from now on," the boy declared.   "I positively will not eat a third helping any more."

"Two's enough, eh, Chet?"   Frank grinned. "Aren't you afraid of starving to death?"

Chet finished his second stack of flapjacks and joined his friends in a stroll around the ranch buildings.   As they neared the bunkhouse, a cheerful voice called out the doorway.

"Mornin'.   Come in.   I got somethin' to show yo'."

It was Terry, the singing cowboy.   He held the door open for them to enter.

"Thar 'tis," he said, pointing.

A long pine table stood in the middle of the cowboys' quarters.   On it lay three piles of range riding clothes.

"Some o' the men kinda got an apology to make," he said.   "Leastways to Frank an' Joe.   We found out from Pye yo' shore c'n ride.   So a few o' us got together some o' our gear for yo'."

"That was mighty nice," Frank said.   "Thanks."

"Pretty swell of you," Joe exclaimed, examining the bright shirts and bandannas.

"We had a little trouble gettin' jeans big enough for yore friend here," Terry said, thumbing toward Chet.

The boys climbed into their new outfits enthusiastically. Chet pulled a wide-brimmed hat rakishly to the side of his head.

"Gimme my six-shooters!" he cried, spreading his feet wide apart and slapping his hips. "Oh, boy, am I sharp!"

The cowboys laughed, and Frank thanked them for their generosity, adding that the Hardys had not expected such treatment from Hank.

"Hank don't know about this," Terry replied, "or his pals Muff an' Red. Just keep it under yore hat, will yo'? Better go. Here comes Hank now."

Chet and the Hardys hastily thanked Terry again and departed from the bunkhouse. Nearing the corral, Chet suddenly wheeled about.

"Gosh, I forgot my bandanna," he exclaimed.

He hotfooted back to the bunkhouse. Terry had gone. The bandanna lay on the floor beside the table.

As Chet leaned down to pick it up, he heard Hank's voice. The foreman was talking on a telephone on the far wall of the bunkhouse. Chet could not help but hear what he was saying.

"Not 'til those wise guys from Bayport **leave,**" the dour cowboy said.

He hung up and turned to go out. Seeing **Chet** standing by the table, Hank became furious.

"Yo' sneakin' coyote!" he roared. "What yo' doin' in here?"

"I c-came for my bandanna," Chet stammered.

"That's a lie," Hank snarled. "Yo're eavesdroppin' on me!"

This was too much for Chet. "What were you saying about us boys?" he demanded.

"None o' yore business!" Hank burst out.

He strode toward Chet and grabbed him by the shirt front. Twisting his fist, he lifted the boy nearly off the floor.

Suddenly Chet remembered! "Don't let anybody push you around," his judo teacher had told him. "Brute strength isn't everything."

The words rang in the boy's ears. Quickly he recalled the armlock grip that Russ Griggs, the ex-Marine, had taught him. With a sudden movement, Chet grasped Hank's left wrist with his right hand. The foreman, caught off balance, relaxed his hold on Chet's shirt.

With another lightninglike move, Chet thrust his left hand under Hank's shoulder, using it as a fulcrum. An agonizing look of pain came over Hank's face as Chet bent the man's arm back. Then, with a flip, Chet hurled the man across the room. Hank teetered backward on his heels, then crashed onto a cot in the corner of the bunkhouse.

Chet could hardly believe his eyes. He had thrown the powerful foreman! Hank regained his feet, roaring for help.

"I'll throw yo' blasted nuisances off this place!" he shouted. "Muff! Red!"

Two cowboys, hearing their boss yell, rushed into the building.

"Grab that guy!" Hank ordered, pointing to Chet. "He tried to murder me!"

Hank's friends advanced on Chet, pinning his arms to his sides.

"What'll we do with him?" one of them asked.

"Tie him to a steer's tail!" Hank thundered.

CHAPTER XV

More Trouble

CHET, frightened stiff, lurched wildly. He managed to throw one of the cowboys off his feet, but the wiry ranchman sprang up, securing a tighter grip on the struggling boy.

"Lemme go!" Chet cried. "Help! Frank! Joe!"

Chet realized he could not pit his strength against three men, judo or no judo. So he quit struggling. Instead he hollered again at the top of his voice.

"Shut up, yo' blubberhead!" Hank growled. "Take him away, men!"

Suddenly the door of the bunkhouse burst open. Frank and Joe rushed in, followed by the singing cowboy.

"Stop!" Frank shouted, seeing his friend about to be kicked by the bellowing foreman.

Hank wheeled. "Yo' stay out o' this!" he snapped at the Hardy boy. "This fat greaser threw me, an' I'm goin' to pay him off!"

"Don't do that, boss," Terry pleaded. "Yo' might hurt him."

"Mind yore own business," the foreman glowered, rushing at Frank. "These kids got no business in the bunkhouse!"

Hank's right hand lashed out at Frank's face. But before it could find its mark the boy grasped Hank's wrist in a vicelike hold.

In a split second the place was in an uproar. Joe rushed at Muff. As he unloosed his hold on the stout boy, Chet tangled with Red.

Arms and legs flew as the Hardys and Chet put all of their judo lessons to practical use. One thud followed another.

Terry stood by, openmouthed. Never before had he seen such a spectacle. Three hardened ranchmen were being set upon by a trio of striplings from the city, and were being beaten. It was unbelievable!

When the smoke of battle cleared, the three cowboys lay in grotesque poses. Hank was draped over a cot. The other two sat on the floor, reclining on their elbows, their legs stretched out V-shaped in front of them.

"Shore is a funny sight," drawled Terry.

All of the scrap was gone from Hank and his henchmen. They pulled themselves to their feet and limped out the back door of the bunkhouse. As Hank left, he turned around and pointed a finger at the boys.

"I'll get yo' for this!" he muttered. "I'm boss around here!"

Terry looked worried. "Hank's a bad actor when he's got a grudge," he said. "I'm warnin' yo' to be keerful o' him."

Suddenly the singing cowboy's mood changed. He reached for his "gee-tar" from his bunk and strummed the instrument. His face broke into a broad smile.

"Listen to this." He grinned. "I'll sing it at the next roundup."

Terry struck a few chords. Then, raising his head high, he burst out:

> "*Thar was a city slicker*
> *Dared grab hold o' foreman Hank.*
> *Oh, yippee, oh!*
> *Now the city kid was quicker,*
> *He had his wits to thank.*
> *So foreman Hank went flyin'*
> *Right clean through the air.*
> *Aye, yi, yah!*
> *I'll remember 'til I'm dyin',*
> *His sad look of beat despair!*"

"Swell!" Joe exclaimed, laughing. "Only I'd advise you not to let Hank hear it."

"How can you make up that stuff so quick?" Chet put in.

Terry scratched his head. "Guess it just comes to me off the range," he answered.

The crooning cowboy remarked that it was time he got started on his chores. The boys walked as far as the corral gate with him, then went toward the house.

"That was nice going, Chet," Frank said, slapping the budding judo artist on the back. "Maybe Hank won't bother us for a while, even with his threats."

"What started the fracas?" Joe asked.

Chet told about the telephone conversation which had ended with a reference to the boys from Bayport, and Hank was not going to do something so long as they were at Crowhead. Frank and Joe scowled.

"So maybe," Chet brightened, "nothing will happen to us while we're here."

"I wouldn't count on that," Joe said.

"Not after yesterday," Frank said. "By the way, we ought to track down that clue."

"Which one?" Joe asked.

"The arrowhead," Frank replied. "The one that nearly hit me in the woods."

"What you going to do with it?" Chet wanted to know.

"I think the tip may contain poison," Frank replied. "Come on, we'll take a look at it."

Joe and Chet followed him to the brothers' room, where Frank had cached the white-feathered arrow. He dipped the tip in a saucer of water for a few seconds, then carefully carried the saucer onto the porch.

A fly buzzed around the water, then settled down to investigate. When it touched the water, the insect keeled over dead!

"Just as I thought!" Frank declared. "But to make sure, I'm going to take the arrow to Santa Fe for analysis."

Frank told his cousin Ruth what he had in mind, then put in a long-distance call to the young pilot who had flown them to Crowhead. Winger happened to be free and promised to come for them at once.

At noon the drone of a plane was heard over the ranch. Winger landed alongside the ranch house and the boys ran to meet him. Frank got in, carrying the arrow wrapped in waxed paper. His brother and Chet followed. Hank saw them from a distance. A queer smile tugged at the corners of his hard mouth.

"There they go," he said to a cowboy standing near by. "I hope they're gone for good!"

When they landed in Santa Fe, Frank, Joe, and Chet went straight to a well-known chemist whose name Ruth Hardy had given them. Frank asked him to analyze the arrow.

"I'll have the report ready in twenty minutes," the chemist said, "if you care to come back."

"Sure will."

The boys left the arrowhead and strolled down the street.

"Let's have a soda," Joe suggested.

"Okay," Frank agreed. "I'm thirsty myself."

They saw a drugstore near by and went in. On a chance, Frank went over to the druggist and asked in a whisper:

"Have you any Arrow cigarettes?"

The druggist, an open-faced and friendly man with a shock of black hair, looked quizzically at the boy.

"Arrow cigarettes?" he said. "Never heard of them."

Frank, feeling sure the man was telling the truth, rejoined Joe and Chet. The three sat on stools at the ice cream and lunch counter. Chet leaned over near the clerk.

"What's that chile con carne on the menu?"

The white-coated youth behind the counter explained that it was red-hot stuff. Chet, thinking the clerk was recommending the peppery food said:

"Gimme some."

The boy took a mouthful, made a wry face, then finished the bowl of chile, after which he put away a double-scoop ice-cream soda. Frank and Joe looked at their friend ruefully.

"You'll be sorry," Joe sang out, when Chet asked for another glass of water.

"Gosh, that chile was hot!" Chet remarked, as the boys rose to return to the laboratory.

When the chemist appeared, Frank hurried over to him.

"What did you find?" he asked excitedly.

"This arrowhead is poisoned," the man replied. "Even a scratch might prove fatal!"

Frank paid the man for his analysis and the three left the place.

"Let's make some more inquiries about Arrow cigarettes," Joe suggested.

They went to one place after another, but none of the proprietors ever had heard of the cigarettes.

"What I want to find out now," Frank said, "is something more about real arrows; Indian arrows."

He spoke to a policeman, who directed the boys to a museum.

"They've got a good collection there," he said.

The trio spent nearly an hour looking over the vast collection. Finally Joe remarked:

"Funny thing. Every one of these arrows is longer than the white-feathered arrows."

"And they're not so thick," Frank added. "Whoever shot at Dad and me makes his own brand of arrows."

"That ought to make it easier to find him," Joe surmised.

After leaving the museum, the boys went back to the Santa Fe airport, where they met Winger.

"All set?" He smiled. After they got in the air, he asked, "Find any more crooked arrows?"

"Not one," Chet replied. "But I had some hot chile. Got any water on this plane? My stomach's on fire." He stuck out his tongue in a panting gesture.

"Sorry. No. Bread would be better, but I haven't any of that, either."

"You'll have to wait until we get back to Crowhead," Joe said. "This will teach you to leave that hot stuff to the Mexicans."

Chet sweated it out all the way back to the ranch. When they arrived, he made a dash to the kitchen.

"Whew!" he said, wiping his brow after three slices of bread. "I think the fire's out now."

After the boys had had supper, Ruth Hardy told them there had been more trouble at the ranch.

"Another cowboy disappeared while you were in Sante Fe," she said. "He took his saddle and all his clothes, just like the other men did."

With their cousin's permission the boys went to the bunkhouse and conducted an exhaustive quiz. The missing cowboy's friends, as well as the rest, could give no explanation for his disappearance. Hank watched the proceedings with slitted eyes, and gave short, negative answers to all questions.

"Do you suppose Hank told them not to say anything?" Joe whispered, as his brother finished the interrogation.

"No," Frank replied. "Cowboys don't talk much, anyway. But I really think they don't know what happened to the guy."

Joe stepped into the middle of the room and addressed the men.

"You fellows ought to know that the disappearance of your buddies is no laughing matter," he said. "The men may be in trouble—serious trouble."

At this remark the lounging ranchers sat up in amazement. A buzz of conversation revealed they had thought the cowboys went off of their own volition to some other ranch, and had said nothing to Mrs. Hardy since they did not want to hurt the widow's feelings.

"I'd advise you to stick to Crowhead," Joe went

on. "And if you value your lives, stay away from the north woods!"

At this admonition, Hank arose from his cot and glared at the Hardys.

"Shut up!" he roared. "I'll not let a couple o' coyotes come in here an' give advice to my men. I'm runnin' the affairs of Crowhead an' I don't need any tenderfeet's help. Now get out!"

To avoid another fracas, the visitors left. Chet thumped Joe on the back.

"Good sermon, Parson Hardy," he said. "Only old die-hard in there didn't like it. Say," he added seriously, "do you think Hank's mixed up in this?"

"He's either guilty as they come," Frank answered, "or else he's the meanest straight guy I've ever met."

"Right," said the other boys together, and Joe added, "I've got an idea. Let's find out how much these fellows know about archery."

"How can we do that?" Chet put in.

"We'll make a bow and some arrows tomorrow," Frank replied, "and let the men try their hand at shooting!"

"I get it!" Chet said eagerly. "Maybe that archer's right on this ranch. Well, count me out. I'll go riding!"

But he did nothing of the sort. The following morning the boys obtained a piece of seasoned hickory from the ranch workshop, and spent several hours on their project.

Frank shaped a bow from it, while Joe and Chet fashioned a couple of arrows.

"We don't need sharp arrowheads," Frank said. "Just make the ends blunt."

That evening, after the cowboys had completed their work, the visitors mingled with them outside the bunkhouse. Frank casually mentioned arrows, crooked and otherwise, and offered to let the ranchmen use the bow the boys had made. A quiet indifference met their suggestion. As one cowboy put it:

"I ain't never had a bow an' arrow in my hands. I'll stake my chips on an old six-shooter any time."

"Well," said Frank, disappointed by the futile attempt to wangle a new clue, "I guess I'll try shooting this thing myself. He strung the bow, inserted an arrow and drew the string back.

Just as he was about to let the shaft fly in the direction of the shed, the Indian Pye rushed up, shouting:

"No shoot! No shoot!"

CHAPTER XVI

Flash Flood

PYE's command not to let the arrow fly was followed by a fearful snorting and bellowing. Frank turned. A mad bull, which had jumped the fence of a shipping pen, was charging directly at him and the other boys.

Quick as lightning, Pye grabbed the bow and arrow from Frank's hands. With one deft, continuous movement, he strung the shaft, drew the bowstring, and let the arrow fly—straight at the bull!

The blunt arrow caught the bull directly between the eyes. He went down in a heap at Pye's feet, stunned by the crashing blow.

"Wow!" Joe exclaimed. "Some shot!"

"You s-saved our lives," Chet stuttered.

Frank was not so jubilant as the others. True, he was thankful that the arrow had found its mark, but the episode raised a serious doubt in his mind about Pye.

Could the apparently friendly Indian be the one who had shot the white-feathered arrows? Pye seemed innocent enough, but Frank was determined to be wary.

The Indian looked sheepish as he handed the bow back to Frank. "Pye not know he can shoot straight any more," he said, grinning.

"You look as if you'd had plenty of practice recently," Frank commented.

Pye looked at the boy in surprise. "I no shoot since boy!" Then suddenly he realized what Frank might mean. "No shoot arrow in woods," he said. "Pye no try kill you."

"That's right," Joe spoke up. "Pye was with me every minute on our ride."

"I'm sorry I doubted you, Pye," Frank said in apology.

One of the men who was preparing to drag the bull away looked up. "What are you all talkin' about?" he asked in alarm.

Before the Hardys could stop Pye, the little Indian excitedly told what had happened to Frank in the woods. The cowboys stared in amazement, then turned their eyes on Joe.

"I see what yo' were drivin' at yestiddy," one of them said. "I shore won't show my face in the north woods!"

As the Hardys and Chet said good night and walked off toward the ranch house, Frank remarked, "We didn't learn much, but I'd like to bet if those woods have anything to do with the missing cowboys, the rest of the men will stay away from them!"

"Sure," said Chet. "And now that you fellows have no more work to do here, we can just have fun."

"What do you suggest, Chet?" Joe asked with a wink at Frank. "A little rope work to snare Arrow Charlie, or—"

"Golly," the boy sighed, "you fellows remember too much. Okay, I'll help you track him down, but don't ask me to hunt for anybody in the north woods."

Next morning the Hardys would have liked to take Pye and Terry and follow the trail of the mysterious archer in the woods, but Hank said gruffly that all his men had to ride fence. The only concession he would make was to permit the visitors to go along with their favorite cowboys.

"We'll meet yo' at the corral," Terry said.

Pye picked out good ponies for the boys. Frank and Joe mounted quickly as Chet struggled to his seat. Then the five riders set off at the tireless trot of the Western range.

They had not gone far before Terry reached to

the left side of the saddle, under his rope, and pulled out a little stringed instrument.

"What's that?" Frank asked in surprise.

"My range gee-tar." Terry smiled. "Regular one's kinda big to tote on horseback. I made this here little fella myself."

As the boys marveled at the tiny guitar, Terry strummed out a melody which kept time with the rhythmic cadence of the trotting pony.

They rode on for several miles, the steady clop-clop of the horses and the rising dust beneath their hoofs almost putting Chet to sleep.

Finally the men's checkup of the cattle brought them not far away from the woods where the arrows had nearly hit Frank. Suddenly the boy reined in his horse.

"What's that sound?" he asked.

"Yo' got good ears," Terry replied. "It's just a bawlin' dogie lost in the woods. Want to give him a hand?"

Pye broke his silence. "Maybe bad man there," he warned. "Me listen." The Indian dismounted and put his ear to the ground. "Hear nothing," he said.

Frank turned his mount into the woods, heading toward the cries of the calf.

"I'll come right back," he called.

The boy rode a hundred yards, then halted to

listen. The bawling of the dogie had ceased, but as Frank sat listening, he spotted something that made his heart leap. At some distance ahead, mounted on a white-faced sorrel in the shadow of a big tree, sat a cowboy. His big Stetson was pulled low over his face, entirely concealing it in the shade of the wide brim.

Frank quelled his first impulse to ride up to the man. Recalling his father's warning, and sure the cowboy was not from Crowhead, he turned his horse around quietly, hurried back to his friends, and reported what he had seen.

"Suppose you four fellows surround the woods," Frank said, "while I question the man. If he has no business on Crowhead property, we'll find out what he's up to."

With the four at their separate stations, Frank rode into the woods again to the place where he had seen the strange rider. He was gone!

The boy made his way to the big tree. The hoof-prints of the intruder's horse were in clear view—and something else, as well.

Excitedly Frank leaped off his pony and bent to the ground. There lay a package of cigarettes. The package was gaily colored in gold, blue, and yellow. Frank picked it up and read "Ramiro Cigarrillos, Mexico."

At the same moment he was startled by the sound

of hoofbeats near the far end of the woods. Frank sprang to his horse and went in hot pursuit of the unseen rider.

In a few minutes he reached the edge of the woods. He could hear the horses of two of his friends, who had taken up the chase. Joe and Terry were racing across the range as if they were trying to break a record. But presently they stopped, wheeled about, and came back.

"He got away," Joe reported, as his horse shook foamy perspiration from its neck.

A distant cloud of dust attested to the fact that the rider, whoever he was, had made his escape on a speedy horse. Pursuit would be futile.

Pye came riding up. "Man go to unhappy ground. Get hurt," he said simply.

"Must have wanted to get away bad," Frank remarked. "I sure wish I'd got a better look at him."

"Where's Chet?" Joe asked suddenly.

"Over there," the Indian answered.

He pointed far to the right of the group, where their friend was seated on his pony, holding both hands to his eyes. Presently he trotted over to where the others had stopped. In his right hand he held binoculars.

"I saw him!" Chet exclaimed jubilantly.

"What did he look like?" Joe asked.

"He was the same guy that came to the farm in Bayport and asked me all those questions!" Chet declared excitedly. "And he was at the El Paso airport. Remember?" Chet looked admiringly at the binoculars and added, "Good thing I asked your cousin Ruth if I could borrow these. Thought I might see something interesting!"

"You sure did!" Joe exclaimed.

"It doesn't leave much doubt," Frank said, "that the person who's making the trouble at Crowhead and the one who's in league with the Bayport thieves is the same man!"

"But what's the connection?" Joe queried. "Do the Arrow cigarette peddlers hide out in this region?"

"Maybe they've got a cabin in the woods," Chet suggested. "That plane may drop them food."

"And Ramiro cigarettes," Frank said. He showed his brother and Chet the pack he had found.

"We're coming back to investigate this place," Joe determined, "and soon!"

The boys started back toward Crowhead. Suddenly Frank exclaimed, "I didn't get that dogie!"

The party headed into the woods again and Frank located the little animal, which had started bawling again. The boy found him mired in a water hole, pulled him out, and let him sprawl across the saddle in front of him.

Terry and Pye started back toward the ranch house, with Joe, Frank, and Chet bringing up the rear. The boys, talking over the actions of the man in the woods, found themselves a long distance behind the others.

Suddenly a black cloud appeared on the horizon as if by magic. The next moment, a torrent of rain was lashing the range.

"We'd better get over this gully onto higher ground," Frank warned.

He led the way into the twisting gulch, on the other side of which was a high knoll. But just when the three boys reached the bed of the gully, a terrifying sound reached their ears. It was a swirling, swishing noise, which reached thunderous proportions as it roared down upon the riders.

The boys were caught in a flash flood!

CHAPTER XVII

The Galloping Archer

THE torrent struck the riders like a gigantic ocean wave.

Frank, choking and spluttering, clung to his mount. The pony struggled with all the rugged strength of a Western animal. Finally, its forelegs beat a tattoo on the bank of the now raging stream, then pulled up to higher ground.

Frank looked around. Farther down the stream Joe was scrambling out of the water, leading a bedraggled pony.

"Where's Chet?" Frank called to him in alarm.

Joe pointed around a bend where he could see an object bobbing like a buoy in the water. Suddenly a hand reached out and grabbed a jutting rock. Then Chet hauled himself slowly to the bank.

The chubby boy looked sorrowful when the others reached him. Pye and Terry had raced back. The storm had ceased as abruptly as it had started, but the water still raged along the arroyo.

"My pony," Chet said, "is dead. She hit something and went under."

"Too bad," Terry said sympathetically. "Lucky none of yo' was hurt."

"You can ride back with me, Chet," Joe offered. "My pony's hefty."

Chet looked ruefully at the stream, which had begun to subside. Then he let out a sudden exclamation.

"What's the matter?" Joe asked.

"Look!" Chet pointed.

All eyes turned upstream, where a white Stetson was floating down. As it spun in the stream, it looked like a miniature carousel stripped of its horses.

Instantly Pye reached to his saddle and grasped his rope. After a few deft turns of the wrist, the Indian let the rope uncoil out over the water. It landed on the Stetson as neatly as a hatband. Pye gently pulled it to shore, where Frank picked it up.

Suddenly he stared in amazement. "The crooked arrow!" he exclaimed.

"Where?" Joe cried excitedly.

"In the hatband," Frank replied.

The other boys scrutinized the Stetson, which had the familiar crooked arrow skillfully burned into the leather.

"And look at this!" Joe added. "The initials inside are C. B. M."

"Arrow Charlie!" Frank burst out, again referring to the name of the man supplying Arrow cigarettes to the criminal trade. Was he the owner of this hat, floating in the arroyo hundreds of miles from the Hardys' home town?

"I'll bet he was the man in the woods!" Joe exclaimed.

The same thought suddenly struck the brothers. It was possible C. B. M. had drowned in the deluge. Frank spoke to Pye and Terry. Silently the group rode along the bank of the arroyo for some distance, but found neither the man nor his horse.

"Guess he escaped," Frank said finally. "And tomorrow I'm going to find out where to!"

When the riders reached Crowhead, Frank asked his cousin Ruth if she knew anyone whose initials were C. B. M.

"I know of no one with those initials," she told him. "But I'll contact the sheriff and ask him."

She went quickly to the telephone, but the sheriff said he had no idea who C. B. M. might be. She decided to ask the state automobile license bureau.

"It's too late to try tonight," Ruth Hardy said, "but I'll do it first thing in the morning."

Cousin Ruth, who knew the man in charge, put in a call to the capital. When she explained the nature of her request, he promised to look through his files and asked her to call back in an hour. The time seemed to drag as they all waited. When the hour was up, Cousin Ruth eagerly put in the call again.

"I'm sorry not to be able to help you," the man said. "Nobody in New Mexico—that is, nobody who drives a car, has the initials C. B. M."

As the widow hung up and reported to her cousins, Joe said with a sigh, "Another blind alley! Just when we think we have a red-hot clue, it turns out to be a fizzle."

"I still think C. B. M. is Arrow Charlie," Frank persisted. "And I believe he's the person who wounded Dad and tried to shoot me!"

"If we could only nab him," Joe said, tightening his lips with determination, "then maybe we could squeeze the truth out of him about these two mysteries."

"I have it!" Frank exclaimed, snapping his fingers. "If Arrow Charlie is an expert archer, let's set a trap for him."

"Swell," Joe replied. "But how?"

"Here's my plan," he said. "There's to be a rodeo at the Circle O Ranch. I saw a poster down in the bunkhouse."

"It starts next week," Joe put in. "But what has that to do with Arrow Charlie?"

"We can put up a prize for an archery contest—a horseback archery shoot."

"Now I get it," Joe said enthusiastically. "Arrow Charlie may sign up and we'll capture him."

"It might not be that easy," Frank cautioned, 'but we can give it a try. What do you think?" he asked his cousin.

"I'll go along on it," she agreed, "and put up a fifty-dollar prize."

The next day Frank rode to the Circle O Ranch to confer with the rodeo manager. After he had explained about his prize for the best horseback archer, the manager was agreeable.

He promised to send out circulars and posters advertising the extra event. Frank and Joe could hardly contain themselves as the day of the rodeo neared. Finally it came, bright and cloudless.

The Hardys and Chet arrived at Circle O an hour before the contests were scheduled to start. Making his way directly to the rodeo manager, Frank asked how many had entered the special archery event.

"Only three," came the disappointing reply. "Guess there ain't many cowboys who can shoot a bow and arrow."

None of them had the initials C. B. M., but Frank was sure, if the man came at all, he would use another name.

Finally the announcer bawled out the announcement of the archery event. A ripple of excitement surged through the crowd. This was something new.

Chet scrutinized the three who entered the ring. One was an Indian, an old and scrawny man. The other two were nondescript cowboys.

"Any of these the one you saw on the white-faced horse?" Frank asked.

"No," he said.

After placing the target, which was a straw-filled dummy with a white paper heart sewed to the jacket, the announcer shouted:

"The winner must pierce the heart, while riding at full gallop! Three shots for each contestant. Let 'er go!"

The first cowboy trotted around the circle, guiding his mount with the pressure of his knees. In his hands he held a bow and across his back was slung a quiver.

Gaining speed, he galloped past the target, taking careful aim. The bowstring zinged, and the arrow flew toward the dummy. It pierced the head as the crowd roared.

The contestant's next shot went wild. The third landed just below the heart.

The next aspirant, the Indian, fared a little better. All his arrows hit the dummy, but none found the heart. Up rode the third man, obviously nervous.

The cowboy strung his bow, bringing his horse to an easy gallop. He handled the bow like an expert, drawing the nock of the arrow back slowly while taking aim.

Suddenly the crowd shrieked. Just as the arrow left the bow, the cowboy's horse stumbled, throwing the rider hard to the ground. The arrow, sent on a wild flight, embedded itself in a fence post.

The cowboy was too shaken to continue. He walked away.

In the excitement that followed, few people noticed a late arrival stride to the judges' stand. The man signed up for the event, bow and arrow in hand. The instant the third contestant had withdrawn from the meet, the newcomer mounted a peppery pony and pranced around the circle. Then, stringing his bow, he galloped toward the target.

"Look!" Joe shouted.

The rider suddenly sprang upright, his feet gripping the saddle. With the ease of a circus rider, the cowboy stood straight, while the horse continued to gallop. With the crowd paying a roaring tribute to his feat, the rider aimed a white-feathered arrow and let it fly. With a thud it cut through the middle of the paper heart!

"Did you see the white feathers?" Joe gasped.

"Let's talk to this guy," Frank said excitedly, pushing his way through the cheering throng.

Suddenly Frank froze in his tracks. The cowboy had continued at a gallop directly to the judges' stand. The rider bent over and scooped up his prize money, which a dumfounded judge held in an envelope.

Then, spurring his mount faster, the archer vaulted a low fence and disappeared over the shimmering prairie in a cloud of dust!

CHAPTER XVIII

Fire in the Woods

"WELL, I'll be a horned toad!" Joe exclaimed as he watched the cloud of dust vanish in the distance.

The archer had ridden off so swiftly, none of the boys had been able to get a good look at his face. Chet said he was not the man they had seen in the woods, however.

Although the trap they had laid so carefully had not been a success, it had not been without a reward. It had produced another white-feathered arrow! Frank, eager to examine it, cried:

"Let's get over to that target pronto, before it's taken away!"

The three boys elbowed their way through the surging rodeo crowd to the spot where the straw-stuffed dummy lay grotesquely on the ground. The arrows were still sticking from it like porcupine quills.

Frank bent down and pulled the winning shaft from the heart of the effigy. After examining it carefully, he turned to Joe.

"It's identical to the other white-feathered arrows."

"Which means," Chet put in, "that the archer who just left this is the same man who shot at you in the woods."

"Maybe yes, maybe no," Frank observed. "But I'm going to find out. This time nobody's going to stop me!"

"How can you do it?" Chet asked.

"We'll go back to the woods," Frank replied, "but this time we'll make it an overnight expedition so we can stay and watch as long as we want to. I think the stone with the crooked arrow on it may even be a meeting place of some kind."

"We'll take Pye and Terry along," Joe said. "That is, if Hank will let us."

"I'll ask him as soon as we get back," Frank said. "Anyway, I want to find out from him if he smokes Ramiro cigarettes. I forgot to ask him."

Frank already had examined the pack and found there were no gas-filled tubes in the cigarettes. So a momentary notion he had that the crooks might have changed the name from Arrow to Ramiro had proved false.

Upon reaching home, the boys rubbed down their

horses, then Frank approached Hank. He was standing alongside the corral smoking a cigarette. Frank explained their proposed venture and asked if Pye and Terry might go along.

"No!" the foreman fairly barked. "Yo' can't take my ranch hands every time yo' a mind to do some sightseein'!"

Frank realized it was useless to argue with the obstinate foreman. The boy turned the subject of conversation to cigarettes, asking what Hank smoked.

"Ramiros," he replied, and stalked off.

"Yo' shore look like a lost dogie," a voice said suddenly. "What's on yore mind?"

Looking up, Frank saw Terry near him. On a hunch the boy asked the singing cowboy what he really thought of Hank.

"Mighty ornery," Terry replied. "But he's loyal to Mis' Hardy, if that's what yo're drivin' at."

"Thanks," Frank said. "See you later."

The boy went straight to Ruth Hardy and brought her up to date on the progress in solving the Crowhead mystery. She backed up Terry a hundred per cent in his conclusion about Hank's honesty. In view of her faith in her foreman's honesty, Frank said nothing of the telephone conversation Chet had overheard in the bunkhouse.

"I'll see what I can do about convincing him to

let Pye and Terry go with you on your ride. I don't want you to go alone."

After dinner she summoned Hank. The boys cleared out when the sullen foreman entered. Their cousin took him into the living room alone, closing the door behind her.

Half an hour later the two emerged, Hank's expression unchanged. But as he strode back to the bunkhouse, Mrs. Hardy came to the boys.

"Everything's fixed up," she said, smiling.

"You mean we get Pye and Terry?" Joe asked quickly.

"They'll ride with you tomorrow," his cousin replied. "Hank didn't want to let them go, because he's so shorthanded. But I told him a day's work wouldn't matter, if we can clear away this cloud that's hanging over the ranch."

It was growing dusk when Frank and Joe went to tell Pye and Terry about the next day's plan. Both were eager for the trip, especially the Indian.

"We track bad hombre Indian way," he said enthusiastically.

"How's that?" Joe asked.

"Use wild animal feet." He grinned. "He no find us."

"How do we get the animals to do that?" Joe asked, laughing.

"You no savvy," Pye replied. "Pye make animal

feet from wood. Tie on bottom of boots. Look like animal track."

The brothers thought Pye was fooling, but next morning, while the boys and Terry were saddling their mounts, Pye ran up to them excitedly.

"Here animal feet," he said proudly.

In his hands he held five pairs of queer-shaped wooden contraptions, with leather thongs for tying them to the boots. "Bear, wolf, fox, wildcat, deer," he identified them.

The Indian handed one pair of "feet" to each rider. The travelers hung them alongside their saddlebags, which were filled with food and cans of tomato juice. Each man carried a blanket secured to the back of his saddle. Presently the five trotted off.

Before they had gone far, Frank noticed that the Indian carried a bow and arrows. They were partly hidden under his rope.

"What you got there, Pye?" he asked, pointing to the weapon.

"Me carry bow and arrows you boy make," Pye answered. "Maybe we shoot. Savvy?"

As on the previous trip, the riders became silent once they had settled down to the long jaunt. At first Terry burst forth with a Western ditty, but as they neared the mysterious woods, even he became quiet.

They went straight to the spot where Frank had seen the mysterious rider.

"He's been back!" the boy exclaimed, dismounting to examine fresh hoofprints.

Marks of a pony were all about the area, indicating the animal had stood and pawed the ground. Where had his master been while the pony waited? Examination proved the rider had not dismounted.

"Let's see where the hoofprints lead to," Joe said.

He and Pye took the lead, with Frank, Terry, and Chet in a row behind. The stout boy glanced fearfully over his shoulder, as if afraid an unseen hand were ready to grab the last man in line.

Picking their way carefully along a sort of trail, the five riders approached an area of sparsely wooded ground, then emerged on the other side of the forest.

"Here's where I saw him get away," Chet announced.

"And here's where we lose him again," Frank declared, examining the hoofprints.

Marks of a horse's hoofs became intermingled with the hoofprints of cows. Soon they were lost in the welter of hundreds of marks made by the roving animals.

But the riders continued on, hoping to pick up the trail. Suddenly Pye reined in.

"What's up?" Frank asked.

"Look! Top trees!" the Indian cried, a note of alarm in his voice.

"It's smoke!" Chet exclaimed.

A blue curl spiraled into the cloudless sky, some miles in the distance.

"Forest fire!" Terry burst out.

Frank and Joe looked at each other. Another tragedy for Cousin Ruth!

CHAPTER XIX

The Dangling Rope

FEAR gripped the hearts of the group from Crowhead. If this were a forest fire, it might spread to the open prairie, consuming miles and miles of pasture grass and timberland as it raced toward the buildings of the ranch.

"I'll ride back and give the alarm," Joe volunteered. "They can get a fire-fighting plane out here to help us."

He wheeled his pony, ready to cover the grueling miles to the ranch house at racing speed.

"Wait!" Terry cried suddenly. Then he added, "What do yo' think o' this, Pye? Forest fire or camp site?"

The Indian stared long and thoughtfully at the curling smoke. He watched for indications of spreading flames but saw none.

"No forest fire," he announced laconically. "Hombre make fire. Cook grub."

As all eyes focused on the smoke, it seemed to fade out, confirming Pye's notion that the blaze was under control.   But under the control of human beings.

"Would any of the Crowhead cowboys be camping there?" Frank asked Pye.

"No cow, no men," the Indian answered.   "Pye tell you bad place over there."

"You've been in that forest?" Frank queried in amazement.

"Pye no go," the man answered.   "Ancestor say stay away, so stay away."

"But what's there to make it bad?" Frank persisted.

The Indian shrugged.   "Pye no know.   But Pye not afraid.   We go see."

"That's the stuff." Frank praised.   "Come on!"

The sun was low as they neared the forbidding forest.   The sky was taking on the vivid, darkening colors of sunset.   Purple and magenta clouds blended into the pink backdrop of the heavens. which were making ready to cloak the plains with darkness.

"We'd better look for a camp site," Frank suggested.

"You got plenty savvy," Pye commented admiringly.   "Dark come in."

After scanning the area, Joe and Terry found a

rocky gulch, protected from the wind and affording an ideal place to spend the night. After tying their animals, the five travelers built a fire in the bottom of the gulch, so that it would not be seen by other campers. Terry said that he and Pye would take turns standing watch during the night.

Frank unpacked the provisions. Putting a tender piece of beef on a spit, he turned it over and over above the fire until its rich juice sizzled a merry tune.

"Hot diggidy!" Chet exclaimed, sniffing the savory odor. "This night air makes me hungrier than ever!"

After they had eaten, the boys set about to make their beds. Frank and Joe quickly dug little depressions to fit the contours of their bodies, arranged their blankets half under them, then crawled in, pulling the rest of the blankets over them. Chet was still digging. Finally he, too, settled down, along with Terry. Pye stood watch until three o'clock when Terry took over.

The sun was sticking its red thatch above the distant horizon when Frank awoke. He shook Joe, then tossed a pebble at Chet. It bounded off the sleeping boy's freckled nose and he sat up with a start.

"Oh, wowee!" he exclaimed. Then, grinning,

he added, "Am I relieved! I dreamed a snake was crawling over me."

"Bad dream," Pye said, shaking his head. The Indian and Terry were busy with breakfast. "Bad luck dream of snake," he prophesied.

"Let's hope it doesn't strike today," Frank remarked. "Gosh, that bacon smells good."

By the time the group had eaten, the sun was ascending like a barrage balloon.

"Let's get going," Frank urged.

"Go slow. Watch for bad hombre and snake," Pye advised.

"S-snakes?" Chet quavered.

"Maybe big chief ancestor mean poison snake," Pye shrugged, as the party advanced cautiously into the forest.

Suddenly the Indian halted the group. He said he thought they had gone far enough on horseback and should investigate further on foot.

"Put on animal feet," he ordered.

The boys tied on the tracking feet. Joe became a fox, Frank a bear, and Chet a wildcat. Pye and Terry strapped on deer and wolf feet. Then they walked stealthily forward, listening intently and looking for clues that might lead them to Arrow Charlie or at least to the men responsible for some of the strange, recent happenings.

But their search proved fruitless, and the going tough. Any campers had covered their tracks well, and any riders to the forest certainly came and went by a totally different route.

Finally the boys and the two Crowhead men returned to their ponies. Just as they were about to mount, the sound of an airplane sifted down through the dense trees. The boys peered up through the heavy foliage but could see nothing.

"Give me your glasses quick, Chet," Joe said.

He looped the strap of the binoculars around his neck and made for a tall tree near by. Shinning up to the first branch, Joe quickly climbed to the top limb. He put the binoculars to his eyes and scanned the countryside.

Presently a small plane came into view. It looked like the same one the boys had seen before. Dangling from it was a long rope. It reached nearly to the treetops as the plane skimmed along.

At the end of the rope was a small package. As Joe glued his vision to it, the plane dipped out of sight behind the upland forest. Joe climbed down to report what he had seen.

"Do you suppose the plane was dropping the package?" Frank asked excitedly.

"Either that, or the pilot had picked it up," Joe replied.

"That proves the smoke did come from a campfire," Terry put in. "An' it can't be far from here."

"Let's go!" Joe cried, eager to be off.

"No go fast," Pye advised. "Enemy of Crow-head maybe plenty smart."

"Pye's right," Frank agreed. "We'd better go on foot."

"An' go separately," Terry said. "It'd be too bad if we all got caught at once."

Heeding the singing cowboy's advice, the five hobbled their ponies and set off in different directions, but all heading generally toward the spot where Joe had seen the plane. They agreed to return to the ponies in two hours.

Frank set off first, creeping along stealthily. After going several hundred yards, he stopped to listen. A little noise came from his left. Probably Chet, Frank thought, but to make sure, he hid himself inside a large, hollow log and waited.

What he saw made his heart pound. A grim-faced Indian was stepping from behind a tree, a bow clutched in his left hand. Five white-feathered arrows poked out from the quiver slung over his shoulder. They were the same as the arrow that had struck Mr. Hardy!

In a panic Frank wondered where the rest of his party were, and hoped they would spot the Indian before he let the arrows fly!

CHAPTER XX

Captured!

THE Indian stopped, as if his sixth sense had detected a human being, and carefully scanned the area. When he failed to see anybody, he stalked on through the woods.

Frank wriggled from his hiding place and followed. Keeping a safe distance from the Indian, Frank tracked him through the dense timberland.

Suddenly the Indian wheeled around. Frank, watching his every move, ducked behind a bush just in time. The man looked left and right. Then he put his ear to the ground. Finally satisfied, he set off again, this time at a ground-covering lope.

Frank matched the Indian's powerful strides. When they had gone about a mile, a trail seemed to appear out of nowhere.

"I wonder where this leads?" the boy thought.

The question was answered a few minutes later. The Indian slowed down to a jog and emerged into a clearing. Frank, breathing heavily from the long run, concealed himself behind a tree.

In front of him lay a small Indian village! Adobe huts stood here and there around the fringes of the open space. In the center were several small work-benches, around which a dozen Indians were work-ing. The man whom Frank had traced disappeared into one of the huts.

"Gosh," Frank said to himself, "this is some surprise! No Indian reservation is supposed to be within a hundred miles of Crowhead. This must be a bunch of renegades!"

Creeping around the edge of the camp, the boy tried to make out what the Indians were doing. He could not tell from their conversation, because the men spoke in their native tongue.

As Frank moved closer, he noticed that one Indian, seated on the ground beside a low bench in the shade of the trees, appeared to be the boss of the other workers. He went now and then to examine the finished products. He carried some of them back to his bench.

Frank watched for a chance to get nearer. When the man walked to the middle of the clearing, the youth quickly stole to his bench.

On it lay leather belts, watch straps, a silver-cased wrist watch, and several silver crooked arrow tie clasps!

Frank stared in amazement. Had he found **the** **head**quarters of the gang?

Maybe this was the reason Arrow Charlie had not wanted Mr. Hardy to come to Crowhead! Whatever these Indians were up to had a direct connection with the gas-filled cigarettes.

Frank scurried into hiding seconds before the leader returned. Then he hurried back toward the place where the searchers had agreed to meet.

The boy had taken note of landmarks along the way to the Indian camp. Nonetheless, it required all his knowledge of woodcraft to find his way through the trackless forest. Finally he neared the point where he had crawled into the hollow log.

Suddenly he heard a noise, like somebody thrashing through the underbrush. Could the Indian be returning? Had they followed his trail?

"They wouldn't be making all that noise," he reasoned.

Confident that the sound did not come from Indians, Frank stealthily made his way toward it. Peering from behind a tree, he let out a low gasp.

"Chet!" he called softly. "For Pete's sake be quiet!"

Chet looked up, startled at the unexpected voice.

"Wh-where did you come from?" the stout boy puffed.

"I heard you kicking around like a lost dogie,"

Frank chided. "You'd better be quiet. There are Indians in these woods."

"Indians!" Chet exclaimed. "First a bear and now Indians!"

"A bear?"

"Yes. A big one just chased me."

In a hushed voice, Frank told him about the hidden Indian camp, and what the men were making. Chet's eyes bulged.

"Let's g-get out of here!" he cried. "Wh-where's my pony? I'm going!"

Despite Frank's efforts to restrain his friend, Chet broke away in a run.

"Stop!" Frank demanded in a hoarse whisper. "You'll get lost again."

Hardly had he uttered this warning, when the twang of a bowstring resounded among the ponderosa pines. An arrow whizzed through the air and embedded itself with an ominous thud in a tree trunk alongside Chet.

Instantly two Indians appeared, running toward Chet, who was frozen with fright. Apparently they had not seen Frank, but the dark-haired boy dashed forward to protect his friend.

The Indians gave a whoop on seeing the second boy. The taller one, well over six feet, ran toward Frank, while the other continued in Chet's direction.

Frank braced himself for the onslaught. The

Indian, a wiry man with bulging muscles, grabbed Frank in a viselike grip.

In a split second Frank broke the grip with judo. The amazed Indian hesitated for a moment, just long enough for Frank to clamp a terrific headlock on him. The Indian struggled, grunting some muffled words, as Frank applied more and more pressure.

But a different scene was taking place alongside the tree where Chet was standing. The Indian who tackled him knocked the wind out of the stocky youth. Chet's judo was useless by the time he had regained his breath.

"Help, Frank, help!" Chet cried.

The Indian sat astride the boy like a cowboy on a bucking bronc. Taking a thong from his belt, he tied Chet's hands behind him, then went to the aid of his companion.

Frank had pinioned his adversary, at the same time watching every move of the other man. When the second Indian was nearly atop him, Frank let the first one go and threw the oncoming one over his shoulder. The man landed with a thud, then bounded up and flung himself at the boy.

In the ensuing struggle, Frank fought like a tiger. It took both Indians to hold the boy down. Finally they managed to tie Frank's hands, and then led him to where Chet was lying.

Chet's teeth were chattering. "S-sorry I let you down," he said.

"Forget it," Frank replied. Then, turning to the Indians, he said, "What are you fellows up to?"

The taller Indian spoke one word.

"Come!"

Walking single file, with one Indian in front and the other bringing up the rear, the boys were led through the forest to the Indian camp. When they appeared in the clearing, the workers excitedly left their benches and crowded around them.

"Plenty strong," the big Indian said, pointing to Frank. "Watch careful."

With the tribe gazing at their captives, Frank asked, "What reservation is this?"

A stony look was the only reply. He spoke to the other Indians in their native tongue, then turned to the boys.

"Follow!" he commanded.

The Indians led the boys a short distance into the woods on the other side of the camp. At the spot stood a well-built, sapling stockade. Frank and Chet were pushed through a crude doorway, which was slammed shut after them.

As the Indians went back to the clearing, the boys heard the leader say:

"Big boss come soon. Fix boys good."

CHAPTER XXI

Wild Dogs

FRANK and Chet looked at each other in dismay. Who was the boss, soon to arrive and pass judgment on them?

"M-maybe he's an Indian Chief," Chet said. "I hope he w-won't burn us at the stake!"

"I doubt that he's an Indian," Frank replied. "The word 'boss' is a white man's lingo."

About an hour later someone approached the door of the stockade and lifted the latch. A stooped, haglike squaw entered. The elderly Indian woman was carrying two bowls, one filled with water, and the other with maize. She set the bowls on the ground, then untied Chet's bonds. Motioning for Chet to free Frank's hands, she slipped out again and secured the door.

"Gosh, she looks like a spook," Frank said. "I'll bet she's over a hundred years old."

With his hands free once more, he joined Chet in a simple meal that tasted much better than they had anticipated.

Hardly had the hungry boys finished, when footsteps sounded outside the stockade. It was the tall Indian, who flung open the door and beckoned to the boys.

As Frank and Chet stepped outside the compound, they were immediately surrounded by an escort of six braves, who marched them silently to an adobe hut.

Stooping to enter the low doorway, the boys found themselves in a dim, candle-lighted room. They uttered a gasp of astonishment. Standing before them was a brawny man whom both boys recognized at once. He was the fellow who had slugged Slow Mo and escaped on the train. And the same one who had quizzed Chet on the farm back home!

Frank's brain raced to piece together the clues of this puzzle, which seemed to be dropping into place with amazing speed. Following a strong hunch, the Hardy boy said defiantly:

"You're C. B. M., otherwise known as Arrow Charlie."

The big man's evil eyes fairly popped. Recovering from his surprise, he managed a crooked smile.

"Yes," he said, "I'm Charlie Morgan. You seem

well acquainted with my alias. Likewise, I'm well aware who you two are."

The boys exchanged troubled glances as Morgan continued, his voice growing louder.

"I know all about you meddling Hardys. And this fat friend of yours here told me everything about your proposed trip to Crowhead."

Arrow Charlie laughed raucously over the easy way in which he had learned of the boys' plans. Chet winced, but Frank shot back defiantly:

"We've found out all about you and your Indians!"

"A lot of good that will do you," Morgan gloated. "You're going to stay here—as my guests—for a long, long time."

"Not when Dad knows we're missing," Frank retorted. "He'll find us!"

"So you think," Morgan shouted. His face grew purple with anger at the mention of Fenton Hardy's name. "Your father's interfered all he's ever going to in my business."

"So you're the one who shot him!" Frank said.

Arrow Charlie smiled evilly.

"No, I didn't shoot your father," he said, "although I'm not a bad shot myself."

"Who did?" the boy demanded.

"One of my men," came the answer. "He's the greatest archer in the world. Nothing but the best for Arrow Charlie! I'll call him and a couple of other friends of mine you should meet." He clapped his hands.

The big man was reveling in the situation. Frank could see he was an egotist and quickly planned to make the most of the man's bragging and acquire some useful information.

"Your Arrow cigarettes were a clever stunt," Frank led him on.

"You like the idea, eh?" Arrow Charlie asked. "Nobody would suspect an innocent-looking cigarette of containing knockout gas. I hear you got a whiff of it, too!"

The adobe hut echoed to Arrow Charlie's guffaws.

"But they'll never find out where I make 'em," he boasted, "and if Fenton Hardy thinks he'll keep on looking—well, another poisoned arrow for him!"

"You wouldn't dare!" Frank said hotly.

"Oh, wouldn't I?" Charlie sneered. "Pretty soon I'm going to stop selling the stuff to crooks. There's a foreign country ready to pay me a king's ransom for my secret."

Into the hut came a man and a woman. Charlie introduced them as his right-hand henchmen; the chief distributors of his product.

"You're the couple who left your car at Slow Mo's garage," Frank shot at them. "Who took the plates and filed off the engine number?"

The man looked at his Indian wife, then said in surprise, "I dunno."

"Why didn't you come back for your car?" Frank asked.

"I did," the man answered, "but Slow Mo was talking to a state trooper, and I thought they was on to us. So what with losing the watch and—"

"I tell that part," the Indian woman interrupted.

It came out that she was the owner of the wrist watch with the broken strap. While she was driving along one day, it had dropped off. She had put the watch and the attached strap in her purse. Her husband later had picked up the other piece and put it into the car's compartment.

Chet, proud of his friend's cleverness, blurted out the whole story of the watch strap. Arrow Charlie was thunderstruck at first, but when the full import of how valuable a clue the strap had been began to dawn on him, he became furious.

"Take these kids away!" he roared to the Indian who had brought them. "If they try to escape, I'll throw you and them into the hissing crack!"

The Indian lost his stalwart demeanor. "I won't fail," he promised.

With that Arrow Charlie pushed the boys through the door. Frank clenched his fists. Nothing would have given him more satisfaction at that moment than to take a swing at the man who had instigated the shooting of his father.

But knowing force would be futile, the boy went back quietly to the stockade with Chet. The door swung shut and the Indian padded away in the growing darkness.

Alone in the solitude of the stockade, Frank and Chet discussed the case of Arrow Charlie.

"If I ever get out of this," Chet wailed, "I'll never open my mouth again to a stranger."

"Skip it," Frank said. "If you hadn't told Arrow Charlie where we were going, he'd have found out some other way."

"Did you hear him mention a hissing crack?" Chet asked. "What's that?"

"I'm trying to figure it out," Frank replied. "Apparently it's something the Indian is afraid of, otherwise he wouldn't have flinched at Charlie's threat. We've got to get out of here, pronto. Dad's in danger of being shot again, and I'm afraid we may lose our own lives."

"How can we go anywhere in the dark?" Chet asked dolefully. "I can hardly see my hand in front of my face. We'd probably only get into worse trouble."

Frank agreed to wait until daylight. But with the dawn came another unpleasant surprise. A pack of dogs was tied next to the stockade. The boys could hear them snapping and growling.

Later in the day the dogs were suddenly released. Judging from their yelps, they were after somebody.

"What about Joe and the cowboys?" Chet asked with anxiety. "Maybe th—the dogs are chasing them!"

CHAPTER XXII

Racing for Aid

In another part of the forest Joe sat under a ponderosa pine tree. Pye squatted beside him. Their ponies were hobbled near by, occasionally swishing their tails.

"I'm worried about Frank and Chet," Joe said as he furrowed his brow.

The Indian stared impassively at the pine needles which blanketed the ground.

"Maybe get lost," he grunted. "No trail in woods."

"And Terry," Joe continued. "Where'd he go?"

After Frank and Chet had failed to show up at the designated meeting place the night before, Joe, Pye, and Terry had set out to look for them. It was then that Terry had suddenly dropped out of sight. No trace of the singing cowboy could be found.

"I wonder," Joe now hazarded a guess, as a frightening thought came to him, "if Terry disappeared like the other cowboys from Crowhead!"

"Maybe bad hombres get him," Pye replied. "But Terry good friend. No savvy why he leave."

"Let's go back to Frank's and Chet's ponies," Joe said, getting up. "Maybe the boys are waiting there."

The two mounted and made their way to the spot. The ponies were there, but the missing boys still had not returned.

Joe dismounted. Reaching into his saddle bag, he drew out a pad and pencil. After hastily writing a note to his brother, saying they would return there again, he tucked one end of it under the saddle of Frank's pony. Then he and Pye set out on the search again, this time skirting the forest.

After they had ridden some distance, the trees became sparser, giving way finally to a bald clearing at the foot of a cliff. Before the eyes of the startled boy and the Indian, a gruesome scene unfolded. From the top of the cliff a lamb, evidently fleeing from some wild animal, came hurtling down toward them. It landed in a broken heap near their ponies. Joe's mount reared up. Pye quieted his animal, then got off to examine the dead lamb.

"No wild sheep in this country," Pye said, looking up at Joe. "Men here. Go find."

With that the Indian picked up the lamb and flung it on his saddle. Joe asked why.

"Maybe need," he remarked without further explanation. Then he added as he mounted, ' Ride in trees. No noise."

Entering the forest again, Joe and Pye picked their way carefully, scanning the dense timberland for any possible sign of Frank and Chet. Suddenly Joe reined in sharply.

"Something moved ahead," he said.

"Go on foot," Pye suggested.

They dismounted, tied their horses and set off quietly. Presently the sound of a harsh voice came to their ears. Peering from behind a thicket, they saw a rider on a white-faced sorrel.

Joe, not more than thirty feet from the man, recognized him immediately. He was the big man he had chased from Slow Mo's garage!

Standing in front of him, looking up at the rider, was Pete, one of Crowhead's missing cowboys! The mounted man was giving him a tongue-lashing.

"You ran away from Crowhead of your own free will," the rider thundered. "But you're not going back of your own free will. Nobody that works for Charlie Morgan ever double-crosses him and gets away with it!"

"Arrow Charlie!" Joe whispered to Pye.

"I won't tell nuthin'," Pete pleaded. "I only

want to git back to cowpunchin'. I warn't made to work in no factory!"

"You know our bargain," Morgan shouted. "I'll give you one more chance to change your mind."

"Listen, Charlie," Pete said, holding his hands out pleadingly, "what'll happen to me if the sheriff catches up with us!"

"Don't worry about sheriffs, or city dicks either," Charlie sneered. "They're a bunch of fools. Fenton Hardy tried to find out about my racket." The crook guffawed loudly. "One of his sons and that fat guy are my prisoners right now!"

Pete leaned against a tree. "Yo're takin' an awful chance, Charlie," he said. "Frank an' Joe's father—"

"That gumshoe artist?" Charlie cried out. "Fenton Hardy is on his way to Crowhead, but he'll never get there. My pilot will make him a prisoner, too."

Morgan looked down at Pete contemptuously.

"Well, have you made up your mind?"

"Shore," Pete replied. "I'm goin' back to Crowhead. Yo' promised not to shoot me."

"Yeah, I did, you sneaking coyote," Morgan spat. "But try to get back to Crowhead. My dogs will take care of that."

"Yore dogs!" Pete exclaimed.

"Yeah. I keep 'em chained, but when they get loose, they go wild!"

Charlie jerked his reins, sending the bit deep into the sorrel's tongue. The animal reared up and wheeled, then galloped off into the woods.

When the hoofbeats of Morgan's horse faded away, Joe and Pye rushed up to Pete. The cowboy's jaw dropped in disbelief.

"Pye!" he cried out. "How'd you git here?"

"We'll tell you later," Joe put in, leading Pete to where their horses were hidden. "Quick! Jump up in back of me."

The cowboy did as he was told. Then Pye and Joe galloped off in the direction of Crowhead. As the three neared one boundary line of the ranch, there came a sudden howling.

"What's that?" Joe cried out.

Pete supplied the answer, terror in his eyes. "Charlie's dogs!"

"Wild dog now!" Pye shouted. "Bad! Kill us!"

"They're gaining!" Joe cried.

The howls of the dogs grew louder. Turning in his saddle, Joe could see the leader of the pack, his fangs bared, bounding toward them.

"We can't outrace those man-killers!" Pete moaned.

CHAPTER XXIII

A Grim Story

THE Indian's face suddenly lighted up.

"Pye fool 'em," he said.

Just how to fool a savage pack of wild dogs already snapping at the heels of the ponies was more than Joe could figure. The fearful howls were deafening.

Like lightning Pye pulled a knife from his belt. He grasped the dead lamb and severed one hind leg. Joe now realized the strategy of the wily Indian.

Pye flung the leg to the snapping dogs. The pack skidded to an abrupt halt, taking time to tear the meat to pieces. Then they renewed their savage pursuit.

Again and again Pye cut pieces from the carcass to delay the dogs. Their yelping grew farther away as the horses gained. When Pye had but one piece left, he shouted to Joe:

"Wait for Pye at fence."

Swerving Cherry, the Indian galloped off at a

tangent, heading for higher ground. The dogs tore after him.

From the distance, Joe and Pete watched spell-bound. Pye guided his pony up a steep butte, as the dogs gained ground. The way was stony and Cherry slipped once on the rocky slope, but Pye urged the animal on.

With her neck straining under the terrific ordeal, Cherry finally reached the top of the bluff. Pye galloped to the far side of it, then tossed the last piece of lamb to the very edge of the cliff.

Meanwhile, the dogs had scrambled to the top of the butte. Their jaws flecked with froth, the charging beasts bounded pell-mell toward the meat.

Too late to check their momentum, half of them tumbled into the abyss below. Their broken bodies crashed onto jagged rocks, ending their bloodthirsty pursuit. The other half seized the piece of lamb. A brutal scrimmage followed, with the largest dog finally shaking the fragment of meat from the rest of the pack and loping off. But his victory was short-lived. The infuriated pack set upon him, then upon one another.

"What a fight!" Joe exclaimed.

"Only three left now," Pete said. "Guess that ends it."

The survivors limped down the slope and stole off into the forest, licking their wounds.

Pye rode into sight a few minutes later.

"You saved our lives!" Joe cried.

The Indian grinned. "Save Pye life too," he said. "Now rest. No ride 'til sun come up."

He, Joe, and Pete sprawled on the grass.

"Tell us what happened to you, Pete," Joe asked the errant cowboy a little later.

Pete lighted a cigarette, inhaled a few deep draughts, and began. One day, when he was riding the range, the cowboy said, a big man had approached him on a white-faced sorrel. The rider beckoned Pete into the woods.

"You're a fool to work at Crowhead," the man, who was Arrow Charlie, had said. "Hank pushes all you guys too hard. How'd you like to work for me? I'll pay you twice as much as you're getting, and it's easy work."

Pete had been surprised, because he had been talking to one of the other men about Hank's sternness. The conclusion had been that Hank was a tough foreman. But for that matter, most foremen were tough, exacting a stiff day's work from their cowpunchers.

Yet Pete had been interested in the stranger's proposition. The extra money surely would come in handy, because he wanted to get married. Charlie seemed to know this.

"What kind o' work is it?" Pete had asked.

"Never you mind," Morgan had said with an expansive smile. "It won't be hard. That I can promise, and in a little while you can leave with your pockets bulging and go marry Kate."

"Yo' know Kate?"

"Sure. Finest girl you could have picked."

That argument alone would have settled the question of Pete's transferring to a new boss, but Charlie had still another argument to clinch the matter.

"Other boys from Crowhead are working for me," Morgan had said. "You don't think they'd stay if they didn't like it, do you?"

The other cowboys from Crowhead had not returned. And because cowboys are free agents, Pete had figured they must like the work.

"Okay," Pete had said. "When do I start?"

"Tomorrow. Bring all your stuff."

Pete had ridden to the outskirts of Crowhead with his gear, which he hid under a flat rock. Then he had unsaddled his pony. With a slap on its rump, Pete had sent the animal back toward the ranch house, and started off on foot to a spot designated by Morgan.

"Where was it?" Joe asked.

"Deep in the pine forest," Pete replied, "at a rock with a crooked arrow on it. Some hombre met me there after I passed yo' in the woods."

The rock with the crooked arrow! That was the

place Frank had stumbled upon—a rendezvous for Arrow Charlie and the deserting cowboys of Crowhead ranch!

"When we saw you running in the woods," Joe said, "why didn't you tell us where you were going?"

Pete looked sheepish. "I was afraid, I guess," he said. ' wanted to work for Morgan, an' he'd warne me not to tell anyone I was comin', 'cause Hank would make trouble."

"So Hank had nothing to do with the disappearance of his men or with Arrow Charlie?"

"No."

A sense of relief swept over Joe. He asked, "What happened when you reached the crooked arrow rock?"

Pete said that the hombre had two ponies and took him to the Indian village. Then a tall Indian had taken him farther into the woods.

"Finally we came to a big cave. My friends were inside, but they didn't look very happy."

"Why?"

"They were makin' phony cigarettes."

"Arrow cigarettes?" Joe asked excitedly.

"Yo' know about 'em?" Pete asked in surprise.

Joe nodded, then asked the cowboy how much he knew about the cigarettes and their distribution.

"Most everythin', I guess. An' I'm shore glad to be rid o' that mess."

Pete went on to say that the plastic tubes were brought to the "factory" and filled there with sleep-producing gas. The cigarette paper was brought also, but the tobacco, a cheap, wild variety, was grown near the factory. Part of the cowboys' work was growing and curing it.

"Every mornin' Morgan or his skinny friend Silver," Pete continued the story, "went to the hissing crack an' got some o' the stuff."

"Hissing crack? What stuff?"

"Yo' know," Pete said. "The gas they fill the tubes with."

Suddenly Pye gasped.

"What's the matter?" Joe asked.

"Bad gas," said the Indian fearfully. "Kill much Indian long time years. No go near. White man never see."

"Morgan an' Silver shore know 'bout it," Pete said. "What is it, anyhow?"

At first Pye was reluctant to tell what he knew only as a legend with the Indians. The hissing crack was located on the side of a sheer rock. From it came a hissing gas that brought instant slumber and eventual death to anybody who ventured near it.

"Morgan must wear a mask," Joe ventured. "And he must have heard the story from some Indian."

"Many moons ago," Pye said, "Indian chief punish bad hombre. Throw him on gas rock."

"Morgan's racket was bad enough," said Pete, "but when I found out he sometimes threw men down there, I decided to run away an' squeal on him."

"You take big chance," Pye grunted. "Now sleep." No one slept, however, and at dawn Pye said, "Go now."

At sunup the group heard a plane. Pete explained that one visited Morgan's place daily, dragging a pickup rope. It scooped up the packages of Arrow cigarettes to take to distant places, and also dropped supplies to the gang.

As he talked, the droning came closer. A sudden fear made Joe's nerves tingle. Was his father a prisoner in the plane? Had Morgan's pilot somehow intercepted the detective and taken him prisoner?

Joe flung himself upon his pony. He would ride back to see if the plane was going to land. But Pye and Pete dissuaded the eager boy.

"Get sheriff," the Indian insisted. "Posse take care bad men."

A moment's sober thought convinced Joe that Pye was right. Pete hopped on behind the boy, and the three moved over the hot stretch of grassy land toward Crowhead. The cow ponies, who seemed to sense their part in bringing aid, covered ground rapidly.

Joe's hopes mounted as they drew closer to Crowhead. Perhaps Morgan's schemes had not been carried out. But there was one of their group still unaccounted for. Terry. *Where* was he?

"See ranch house soon," Pye said, sensing the boy's anxiety.

They clopped up a long grade toward the summit of a grassy hill. The ranch was on the other side.

Joe spurred his pony gently. It pulled ahead of Cherry, reaching the brow of the hill first.

Joe gazed at the far-off buildings, then he and Pete cried out in dismay.

"Pye!" Joe shouted.

The Indian raced to the boy's side. Together the three watched as black smoke billowed up in the distance.

The ranch buildings were on fire!

"Probably Morgan's fiendishness!" Joe thought, his jaws set in rage. "Come on, Pye," he shouted, "before it's too late!"

CHAPTER XXIV

The Empty Stockade

By THE time the galloping ponies reached Crow-head, the place was an inferno. Cowhands were running a hose to the ranch house, but the stream suddenly dribbled and stopped as the fire disabled the water pump. Joe rushed up to his cousin Ruth who stood back from the scorching heat of the blaze. Hiding her head in her hands, she sobbed bitterly at this final, crushing blow.

"Joe!" she cried.

"I'm so sorry. I—"

"It doesn't matter so much as you boys," she interrupted. "You're here! You're safe!" She embraced Joe hysterically. "I thought when you didn't come back, something had happened to you!"

The distraught woman did not seem to notice that Frank was not with him. Joe decided not to tell her, but instead to help the men fight the fire.

The loyal cowhands were working frantically. When the pump failed, they had formed a bucket brigade and were passing pails of water from a well up to the blaze.

The man standing nearest the fire was Hank. He looked ludicrous with his eyebrows singed off, his face blackened by the smoke, and his shirt ripped. But the foreman worked like a demon.

Joe dashed up to Pye and Pete. The three formed a new bucket line, and worked on a wing of the ranch house, which was still intact.

Finally the fire burned out. Only the small wing had been saved. Their backs and arms aching, and their bodies scorched by the heat, the cowhands flopped to the ground.

Hank came up to Joe, their eyes meeting for a long moment. "Good work," the foreman said, offering his hand.

Joe shook it.

"Hank," he said, "anybody who fights for Cousin Ruth's interest as you just did is a square shooter. I'm sorry I was ever suspicious of your loyalty."

"Forget it."

"Okay. But there's one thing I'd like to know. What about the mysterious telephone call that Chet overheard in the bunkhouse?"

"Oh, that." Hank grinned. "My brother down

in Albuquerque wanted me to come inspect some cattle, but I didn't hanker to go 'til you boys left. Kinda figgered you might get into trouble."

"We're in trouble right now," Joe told him.

Much as he disliked to tell Ruth Hardy any further disturbing news, Joe knew that not a moment should be lost in trying to rescue his father, Frank, Chet, and Terry.

"I must phone for help!" Joe said after telling his story to her and Hank.

The telephone was in the undamaged wing of the ranch house, but the line was dead. Joe soon discovered the reason. The pole on which the wires were strung had burned to the ground.

There was only one thing to do. Joe must ride to the nearest town for the sheriff.

"I'll go with you," Hank offered.

But no sooner were he and Joe in the saddle than a thundering of hoofs sounded in the distance. It came closer. Soon a group of about thirty riders galloped up.

Leading them was Terry, the singing cowboy! Beside him rode the sheriff!

"Terry!" Joe shouted. "We thought you were lost."

"Say, what's agoin' on here?" the cowboy cried, seeing the smoldering ruins. Then he added,

"That's what Charlie Morgan must 'a' meant 'bout gettin' rid of everythin' at Crowhead. Wal, he shore can't get away with this!"

Suddenly he spied Pete, and stared dumfounded. Quickly stories were exchanged. Terry, while in the woods, had almost run into Arrow Charlie.

"He was talkin' to some skinny guy. They was tryin' to decide what to do with Frank an' Chet, so I vamoosed, pronto, to get help. An' I ain't waitin'. Come on, men!"

"Not without me!" cried Hank. "If them varmints set this here fire an' tried to destroy Crowhead, I'll take the sneakin' coyotes one by one, an'—"

His threat was lost in the noise of men and horses eager to be off on the chase. Joe insisted upon going with the posse, as well as Pye and Pete. When they all had mounted fresh ponies, Hank rode up to Ruth Hardy.

"I know yo're worried about your kin," he said kindly. "But I'm goin' to rescue Frank an' Chet if I have to do it singlehanded. Never knew finer city dudes!"

As the posse was about to gallop off, an airplane motor sounded in the distance. Joe's eyes focused on the speck in the sky. It was coming from the direction of Morgan's Indian camp.

Suddenly a sickening fear seized Joe. Could it be Arrow Charlie's plane? Perhaps it was armed! The posse would be a perfect target for an aerial strafing!

The plane swooped low over the smoking ruins. Then it banked sharply, came in for a landing, and taxied up to the group. As the door of the plane swung open, Fenton Hardy and Sam Radley stepped out.

"Dad!" Joe shouted.

The detective was not one to display his emotions. But the sight of his son gave him a thrill he could not conceal.

"Joe!" he cried as the boy jumped from his horse and raced to his father's side. "I'm glad you're safe. Ruth phoned me you were missing."

Then the sleuth took in the assemblage of riders with a quick glance and his face became grave.

"Where's Frank?"

With Sam Radley listening intently, Joe told why the posse had been organized.

"Sam and I'll go with you," Mr. Hardy said.

As Joe protested, his father told him he had recovered completely from the effects of the poisoned arrow and riding would not bother his leg, which was practically well.

"But first I must send a radio message," he said.

He unfolded a map and Joe pointed out Morgan's

hide-out. Mr. Hardy gave the location to the Federal agent.

"Come quickly," he urged. "There's going to be trouble."

Then the party set off. As Mr. Hardy and the others raced across the range, he brought Joe up to date on the mystery. Morgan's pilot had tried to capture him but failed. Unfortunately, the man was still at large.

The archer who had shot Mr. Hardy was the same man who had tried to steal the car from Slow Mo's, after Frank and Joe had prevented Arrow Charlie from taking it.

"What about the license plates and the defaced engine number?" Joe shouted above the drumbeat of hoofs.

His father said that Bearcat, the man who had sold Frank the Arrow cigarette in Mike's Place, was the culprit. Bearcat had stolen a car. Having learned from Al about the sedan the crooks had left at Slow Mo's garage, he went there, helped himself to the plates to use on the stolen car, and filed off the engine number to forestall its identification.

Many miles had passed beneath the flying hoofs as Mr. Hardy told his story. With Pete leading the way, the party headed toward the Indian camp by a short cut now familiar to Pete.

After a while the trees thinned out, giving way to the clearing of the Indian village. The riders dashed among the adobe huts and workbenches.

But not a move nor a sound issued from the camp. They searched every hut. Bare! The stockade was empty. The place was totally deserted!

CHAPTER XXV

The Roundup

THE Indian village showed unmistakable signs of a sudden evacuation. Ashes in the burned out campfire were still warm, and a few implements were strewn about the workbenches.

"Must have been tipped off we were coming," the sheriff said.

"I think I know how," Joe declared. "The fellow in the plane had binoculars and saw Pete."

"He may even have radioed Arrow Charlie," Mr. Hardy said. "The question is, where are Frank and Chet?"

"I believe they've gone to the caves," Pete spoke up.

"Can you lead us there?" the sheriff asked. "Shore."

The posse headed up the side of the pine mountain after Pete's pony. The way became tortuous as the woods thinned out near the timber line. Joe noticed fresh hoofprints in the stony ground, indicating that ponies had passed that way not too long before. Finally Pete stopped the posse.

"The caves are up there," Pete said, pointing to a winding path, which disappeared around a bend in the mountain.

"Then we'll go on foot the rest of the way," the sheriff said.

Once around the bend, the posse glimpsed the formidable redoubts of Arrow Charlie Morgan's band. A sheer rock loomed high into the sky. At its base a series of deep caves opened up like the sunken eye sockets of a skull.

"We'll go in an' shoot 'em out!" the sheriff declared gruffly.

"Would you mind trying another plan first?" put in Mr. Hardy. The detective was not one to use a gun if a ruse would work as well. He had gained his reputation by clever methods, taking his prisoners alive and unhurt, even if not too happy over falling into Fenton Hardy's traps.

"I have some gas here," Mr. Hardy said. He reached into his pockets and pulled out a couple of gas bombs. They looked for all the world like fountain pens.

"They pack a lot of tear gas," he said. "I think it's time Morgan and his gang did a little weeping."

"That might work in some o' the caves," Pete put in. "But one of 'em has two openings."

The cowboy told how Morgan's men had spent many days working on an escape route for Morgan, if ever such an occasion as this should arise. They had blasted a tunnel from one of the caves right up to the flat top of the big rock. From the top of the rock, Morgan could command the trail with a rifle until his plane, especially equipped for ground pickup, could snatch him up away from any pursuers.

Upon learning this, Mr. Hardy, the sheriff, Joe, and Pete went into a huddle to plan the attack.

"I must rescue Frank and Chet first," Mr. Hardy insisted. "I'll go in alone, with the rest of you covering my advance."

"Not without me!" Joe declared.

Mr. Hardy tried to talk his son out of it, but Joe was adamant.

"Frank's in trouble," Joe insisted, "and we stick together."

The detective agreed that he and Joe should enter the caves first. They would use the tear gas to ferret out the gang when they thought it advisable.

The Hardys advanced cautiously. When they reached the big rock, they flattened themselves out against it. Hearing nothing, they entered the first cave. It was damp and cold. A large rock stood upright in the middle.

Suddenly the sound of muffled voices came from behind it. Joe and Mr. Hardy listened, then advanced noiselessly. Joe flattened himself on the ground to avoid a direct attack, and peered around the big rock.

"Frank!" he exclaimed hoarsely. "Chet!"

Mr. Hardy rushed to Joe's side. On the ground in front of them, trussed with strong ropes, were the two kidnaped boys. Their legs were doubled up and their hands tied behind their backs. Handkerchiefs were fastened across their mouths, making it difficult for them to speak.

Quickly freed, Frank and Chet rose from their cramped positions and stretched. They told how they had been hustled from the stockade the evening before and half dragged to the caves, because there were not enough horses to accommodate everybody at the Indian camp.

Despite their low tones, the group was discovered by a cowboy deeper in the cave. He ran out, a bow in hand. Over his shoulder was slung a quiver. Protruding from it were half a dozen white feather-tipped arrows.

He stood transfixed for a moment. Then he shouted:

"Fenton Hardy!"

"You're the one who shot my father!" Joe cried out.

"Yo' can't prove it!"

"We sure can," said Frank. "And you're the archer who took the prize at the rodeo."

"Yo' bet I am!" the fellow bragged. Then he realized he had identified himself. Furious, he yelled, "I'll fix yo' for good, you meddlin' dick!"

The archer reached back for an arrow, but before he could draw one out, Mr. Hardy grasped the man's wrist, twisting it with such force that the fellow fell flat on his back.

As he did so, the cowboy lashed out with his feet. In a flash the detective gripped one of his boots and applied the toehold until the man yelled in pain. Using the rope that had tied his brother, Joe bound the man's hands.

By this time, Morgan's men had come running from every direction. Mr. Hardy hurried to the entrance of the cave and gave the signal to the posse. They rushed forward, grappling with the cowboys and Indians who swarmed from the caves like ants. The cowboys, who had run away from Crowhead to join Morgan, gave up without a struggle. But the Indians put up a stiff battle. When the dust had cleared, Morgan was nowhere in sight.

"I know where he is," Pete volunteered, and led the Hardys and the sheriff to a cave far back from the others. It was the one with the passageway to the top of the rock.

"Come out, Morgan!" the sheriff roared into the cave.

"Come and get me!" a voice replied, echoing hollowly in the gloomy vault.

Mr. Hardy slipped inside. As he did, a rifle cracked, and a bullet ricocheted off the rocky wall. The detective ducked, at the same time throwing a tear gas bomb into the interior.

Morgan coughed. Then the cave echoed to his fleeing footsteps as he dashed through the tunnel. Mr. Hardy could not follow immediately into the fumes.

Soon Arrow Charlie appeared for an instant high on the roof of the rock. When the men saw the rifle in his hands they fell behind the rocks for cover. He took a couple of pot shots, then from behind a rock sneered·

"Thought you had me, eh? Well, you won't get me. I've radioed my pilot. He'll soon be here to pick me up. Then look out, Fenton Hardy and sons!"

As he spoke, there came the sound of a plane. Frank and Joe listened intently. Was it Morgan's private plane, coming to snatch the criminal from their grip the moment they had him nearly cornered?

"A flying banana!" Joe cried.

"A government helicopter!" Frank exclaimed.

The craft flew close, and descended. Morgan raised his rifle, but before he could fire a shot, a machine gun from the helicopter sent a burst that nicked the rock a few feet from him.

Charlie Morgan knew he was licked. He dropped his rifle and held his hands high as the helicopter landed near him and Federal men hopped out. Mr. Hardy and Sam Radley raced through the tunnel to greet them.

"Swell job, Hardy," said one of the agents. "We've been looking for this guy a long time."

"The credit should go to my sons." The famous detective smiled. "Come and meet them."

Just then another motor sounded high over the big rock. It was Morgan's plane. The pilot swooped low enough to see what had happened, and sped off. But his escape was short-lived. He was captured a few miles away when he was forced to make a landing. Joe and Frank identified him as the pilot who had wanted to charge them the exorbitant sum of two thousand dollars to fly them from Bayport.

When all the prisoners were rounded up, the Federal agents and Mr. Hardy interrogated Arrow

Charlie with a flood of questions. The big man, surly at first, finally realized further silence was useless.

He showed the officers into a secret room deep in one of the caves, where the Arrow cigarettes were made.

"What about the hissing crack?" Frank asked.

Morgan led them to a pit a hundred yards back of the big rock. From one side of it a white plume of smoke hissed out through a split in the rock's surface. Arrow Charlie had learned of the gas from some renegade Indians and had taken a chemist to help him exploit the mysterious fumes.

He had hired the Indians to guard the approaches to his cigarette factory. Then, when he needed more labor, he had lured the cowboys away from Crowhead, the nearest ranch. The Federal men immediately took over the hissing crack and posted a guard around it.

"How did you hit upon the crooked arrow as a sign of identification among your men?" Mr. Hardy asked Morgan.

"That really wasn't an arrow," Morgan replied. "It was an ancient, writhing snake with crooked fangs and a forked tail. I found it carved on a rock pointing to the hissing crack. Must have been put there long ago by Indians as a warning. At first I thought it was a crooked arrow, and decided it would make a swell insignia for my distributors."

On the long ride back to Crowhead, Mr. Hardy, his two sons, and Chet talked over the events leading to the roundup of the Morgan mob. Frank and Chet told how they had been captured.

"That guy who shot you, Dad," Frank said, "was reared by Indians. Morgan sent him to Bayport to shoot you. The same fellow nearly winged me when I discovered the sign of the crooked arrow in the rendezvous rock."

The errant cowboys, reticent at first, began talking on the ride back. When they heard that the ranch had been burned at the direction of Arrow Charlie, they were enraged.

"I think," Pete said, "that we ought to show our hearts are in the right place by helpin' to rebuild Crowhead."

Cheers greeted his suggestion.

"And we won't take a cent," shouted another of the runaways.

For the next two weeks the place resounded to the sound of hammers and saws as the buildings were replaced. Ruth Hardy's appreciation was unbounded.

Then one day, their job done, the Hardys, Chet Morton, and Sam Radley stepped aboard a big air liner to fly home. Frank and Joe felt let down. Life was beginning to seem slow already. But not for long. "The Secret of the Lost Tunnel" was soon to come their way.

When the plane was in the stratosphere and all were settled comfortably, Frank remarked, "I wonder what Slow Mo will say when we tell him we started solving the mystery of the crooked arrow right in his garage."

Joe grinned broadly. "He'll say, 'I never thought of that!'"